THE TELEPHONE GIRLS

THE LILY BAKER SERIES BOOK 2

PATRICIA MCBRIDE

Boldwood

First published in 2019. This edition first published in Great Britain in 2024 by Boldwood Books Ltd.

Copyright © Patricia McBride, 2019

Cover Design by Colin Thomas

Cover Photography: Alamy and Colin Thomas

The moral right of Patricia McBride to be identified as the author of this work has been asserted in accordance with the Copyright, Designs and Patents Act 1988.

Every effort has been made to obtain the necessary permissions with reference to copyright material, both illustrative and quoted. We apologise for any omissions in this respect and will be pleased to make the appropriate acknowledgements in any future edition.

A CIP catalogue record for this book is available from the British Library.

Paperback ISBN 978-1-83561-678-9

Large Print ISBN 978-1-83561-677-2

Hardback ISBN 978-1-83561-676-5

Ebook ISBN 978-1-83561-679-6

Kindle ISBN 978-1-83561-680-2

Audio CD ISBN 978-1-83561-671-0

MP3 CD ISBN 978-1-83561-672-7

Digital audio download ISBN 978-1-83561-675-8

Boldwood Books Ltd
23 Bowerdean Street
London SW6 3TN
www.boldwoodbooks.com

To my husband Rick, and my lovely family

further than Cardiff
her eye. 'Just imagine,
tidy, it is.'
Tidy? How'd you mean?'
. 'I forget not everyone
watch that. Tidy means it's
s, French food, though I'm
her version of.'
been further than London. I
school and looking at the
ed to dream about a honey-
-Super-Mare, which was all
aged, if that. I knew Edward's
urs, but didn't know if he could
able to save something from my
shillings a week and I wanted to
. At least our board and lodgings

ench,' I said.
alt and I stood up for a minute,
peered out of the window. It was a
to hang lifeless in the air with just the
sky peeking through. All I saw were
edges. Snaking ahead, was the front of
ut no sign of what was holding us up.
the train started again. I staggered and
d floor jarring my back. Wriggling to get
h rumbled, and I got out the packet of
me before I left. One was cheese and one
wo of her lovely scones as well, bless her.
'Have you got anything to eat?' I asked.
te them on the first train. Been travelling for

1

MY NEW LIFE BEGINS...

Leaning from the train window, I waved goodbye to Edward, the man I'd been engaged to for less than an hour. The smoke from the engine made my eyes water and I blinked away the little black specks that flew everywhere. I stood for a minute, even after he was lost from sight, wishing he was still with me and reluctant to start my new life without him. Brushing a tear from my eye, I picked up my case and struggled along the corridor, full of conflicting emotions. I wanted to be with Edward, but I'd joined the Auxiliary Territorial Army because I wanted to do my bit for Blighty. Marriage would have to wait. We had our whole lives ahead of us.

But what if he's killed? a wicked voice inside my head taunted.

'He won't be!' I said out loud, and got a funny look from a woman next to me.

I pushed my way past dozens of soldiers standing in the corridors, several times tripping over their kitbags. Each time, one of them helped me right myself with a cheeky comment or a wink; their cheerfulness lifting my mood. But none of them looked as good in uniform as my fiancé. I'd never called anyone that before, and it felt very special.

With aching feet, I walked the whole length of the train, but there were no free seats anywhere.

'Come and sit by yere,' a voice said, just as I was f The girl was about my age and sitting on a ca with a smile.

'Room for a couple of little 'uns like us in t. said. I had to smile back. Even sitting down, it w wasn't little. Slim, yes, but a good bit taller than my inches. She shuffled along, making a bit more room fc her. I put down my small case and leaned against it, I handbag on my knee.

'I'm Bronwyn, from Swansea,' she said, holding out he 'Bet you'd never guess from my accent!'

I shook her hand. 'I'm Lily, from Oxford. Before you ask, n not a clever clogs from the university. I bet you can tell that I my accent.'

'No, you don't sound like a nob,' she said, grinning, 'Where'r you going? I'm off to Aldershot to start ATS training.'

My jaw dropped. 'You're never! I am, too. We'll be training together then. I'm terrified – never been away from home before. I'm so glad to meet you. At least I'll know one person now.'

The train stopped with a sudden lurch that threw us against each other. We looked up, but no one was taking any notice. 'We'll probably be hours late,' Bronwyn said, 'timetables have gone haywire since this war started.'

'Do you think we'll be in trouble? Can they put us on a charge because we're late?'

She laughed. 'Well, they'd have everyone on a charge if that was the case, like. Mind you, we're not properly part of the army yet, so I don't know how that works out. No, they must be used to people being late. Anyway, they're meeting us at the station, aren't they?'

4

France. Maybe even Paris. I've never beer before today.' She got a faraway gaze in Paris! I got a book out of the library and it's I began to think I'd need a translator. ' She laughed and slapped her han speaks like we do in Swansea. Have to v really nice. Eiffel Tower, lovely building used to that because Ma cooks it. Well, I went into a daydream. I'd never remembered learning about Paris a pictures, wishing I was there. I star moon in Paris. That'd beat Westo most people round our way man family were a lot better off than o afford Paris. I wondered if I'd be ATS pay. We were to get eleven send some to my mum regularl wouldn't cost anything. Paris... 'Maybe you can teach me Fr The train ground to a h stretched my aching back an dull day, grey clouds seemed occasional break and blue empty fields bordered by h the train, smoke belching, I Then, with a shudder, quickly sat down, the har comfortable, my stomac sandwiches Mum made fish paste. She'd put in I unwrapped them 'I did have, but I a

ho. in tl not lc nastine 'So w I asked. 'You dor

hours already.' Bronwyn tried not to look at my sandwiches, but I could see she was hungry.

I held the sandwiches out to her. 'Come on, we'll share. My mum always makes me too much.'

We sat silently eating, lost in our own thoughts. Bronwyn brushed crumbs off her coat. 'You sorry to be leaving home?' she asked.

'Yes, I'll miss my mum but you'll never guess what! I just got engaged! I've been bursting to tell someone. My boyfriend proposed just now at the station and I said yes.' I flashed my ring in her face like a right show-off.

She took my hand and studied the ring. 'Fair play now, that's a lovely ring. Must've cost a bit, mind. You're a lucky girl.'

My smile said it all. 'I am, Edward's lovely. He's a soldier too, like we'll be. Well, I suppose we're volunteers really, but you know what I mean. The ring belonged to his grandmother. But I've told him we can't get married until this war ends, because I want to do my bit and they'll probably throw me out if I get married, especially if I get in the family way.'

'That's for sure, better safe than sorry. I've seen too many of my friends get up the duff before they got married. Lads usually cleared off double quick and left them in the lurch, too.'

I blinked hard. 'Oh, I wouldn't do that sort of thing before we're married.'

She shrugged and reached for a scone. Without thinking I slapped her hand and she dropped the scone as if it would burn her. Then I realised what I'd done. 'I'm so sorry, I shouldn't have slapped your hand. Of course you can have it. Acting like my dad there.'

'In my family if you don't grab food first, you won't get any. It's everyone for themselves. Habits take a while to change, but I'll be glad not to need that one.'

'You got a lad pining for you back in Swansea?'

She shook her head. 'No, don't bother with them much. My mum's had bad luck with men and it's put me off. Anyway, what with working in the factory and helping to babysit my little brothers and sisters, there wasn't much time for courting.' She took a bite of the scone as if to say that's enough of that topic.

As well as my mum and Edward, I was missing my best friend Jean. She'd gone to train as a nurse with the Queen Alexandra's a few weeks back. I wondered if our paths would ever cross before this war was over. Maybe Bronwyn would be my new friend, now we were both training together.

* * *

'Wait in here!' the section leader shouted over the noise of the train pulling out of Aldershot station. 'We've got to wait for our transport, then we'll all be on our way together.'

She shepherded us into a cold, bleak waiting room. The walls were painted green to waist height then yellow above. Wooden benches lined either wall. There was a fireplace but it looked like it had never warmed anyone. We all took seats and looked about awkwardly. No one said anything for a minute or two, then Bronwyn broke the silence.

'Hello, everyone, you all going to ATS training?' she asked.

Some said yes, others just nodded.

'Well, we're going to get to know each other. I've heard there's twenty-five girls to a bunkhouse so we'll probably be sleeping together, too.'

Someone giggled.

Bronwyn grinned. 'Oops, didn't mean it like that though. I'm Bronwyn from Swansea and this is my friend Lily who's from Oxford.' She waved her hand at me and I was glad she considered me her friend. The girl next to her was tall, taller even than Bronwyn, blonde and what they call willowy. Her clothes were expensive and her shoes very smart and not a bit practical. She was wearing a floral-print dress with padded shoulders, white lace gloves and a little hat at a jaunty angle. In fact, she was smarter than the rest of us put together.

She gave a strained smile. 'Hello, everyone, I'm Amanda Beauchamps.'

''Ere, you the one what's a lady, got a title an' that?' the girl who giggled said. 'I 'eard a rumour there was going to be a toff training the same time as us.'

'Wherever did you hear that?' Amanda said. 'Loose talk and all that.'

I noticed she didn't really answer the question, and she didn't have time to because the door opened and the section leader came back in. 'Right, everyone, start getting in the lorry out the front.' Her voice brooked no argument.

Ten minutes later, fifteen of us were in the back of an open-top lorry, sitting on hard wooden benches down the sides. It was a bit cold, but the air was fresh after the stuffy train and waiting room. We passed pretty villages with thatched cottages, ancient churches and water pumps on the village green. We gazed at farms where the farmer calling in the cows for milking, and isolated cottages that seemed like they'd fall apart any minute. Once or twice we smelled bonfires and saw curls of smoke meandering in the air lazily, nonchalantly. The girls from the country took it all in their stride, but us townies kept pointing things out to each other like excited schoolchildren.

Finally, we came to the gates of the training camp. Driving through, no one took any notice of us, they were all far too busy, but we gaped like children in a fairground. Groups of soldiers, sometimes men and sometimes women, were rushing here and there. They unrolled and rolled up fire hoses; they rushed about with food ready to be prepared for meals; they carried buckets from one place to another or swept the concrete with the biggest brooms I'd ever seen; and some rolled big guns from one place to another. Three groups practised marching, each one shouted at by their sergeants. The noise was so deafening I wanted to cover my ears with my hands.

'Hey,' I said, 'some of those girls are wearing half uniform, half their own clothes. What's that all about?'

'Perhaps they ran out of clothes that would fit different sizes,' Bronwyn said, 'Do you think we'll ever be able to march like them?'

Amanda nodded. 'I feel exhausted just looking at them. I wonder how long they give us to settle in before we have to do this lot?'

'Till six o'clock tomorrow morning, so don't get too cosy,' Bronwyn said. 'I know 'cos one of my friends has been through this. It's really hard work.'

We climbed down from the lorry and grabbed our suitcases, stiff from all the bumping over country roads. 'Kitbags from now on, girls,' the sergeant commented.

We were shown into a big wooden hut that had twenty-five single beds lined up against the walls. They were narrow, about two feet wide. I ran my hand over the bedding waiting to be made up. It was scratchy and uninviting. There was one pillow per bed. The beds had metal folding legs and beside each one was a small cupboard for our stuff.

A different section leader appeared as we were getting settled in. 'Welcome, everyone,' she said, 'I'm Section Leader Johnson, but you can call me Miss Johnson. Male army officers will be taking you for square bashing, PE and most lectures. You must be sure to use their rank when speaking to them. I'm going to be looking after you for the next six weeks. Any problems other than missing your mums, come to me and I'll see what I can do. Now, make yourself at home and let's meet outside in five minutes to get your medicals done and then collect your uniform.'

I nodded to Bronwyn and we headed towards the beds nearest the wood-burning stove which seemed to be the only source of heating in the hut.

'Must be a bit different from what Lady Amanda's used to,' she whispered.

I put my finger to my lips. 'Shh, it's not what I'm used to either. We're not posh, but I haven't got any brothers or sisters so I've got the box room to myself.'

She raised her eyebrows. 'And you think you're not posh! I share a bedroom with two sisters and a brother. We all sleep in the same bed, top to tail. It's a double, mind. They wriggle something terrible and the boys can fart for Wales. We keep each other warm in winter though.'

Some girls were looking around the room with dismay, while others were already unpacking and trying to fit all their stuff into their little cupboard. I noticed the time. 'We'd better go!' I shouted.

'Okay, boss!' someone shouted back. 'You goodie two-shoes or something?' But it was said with a laugh.

Miss Johnson was waiting outside for us.

'Before we go to the medical officer and then the quartermaster for your uniforms, let me show you the ablutions. That's what the army calls the bathroom,' she said. 'This way.'

It was a long, cold room with twelve washbasins and three toilet cubicles.

'Where's the bath?' Amanda asked with a frown.

'No baths, you have to manage with the sink,' Miss Johnson said.

'What, strip wash in front of everyone?' Amanda was blinking rapidly.

'No privacy in the army, dear.'

Immediately there was a groundswell of complaints, including from me. As poor as my family were, we gave each other privacy, even in the days when we had to use a tin bath in the kitchen. I quailed at the thought of stripping off in front of everyone. Then I thought of the men fighting in the war. They had much worse things to worry about. I decided to just get on with it and not worry about my modesty. After all, we were all girls.

The medicals and injections were brief, but meant a lot of waiting around. That gave us a chance to get to know each other better. I quickly found some girls I liked and a few I decided to avoid.

We needed a sense of humour when we got our uniforms. Each of us got two pairs of striped pyjamas, two bright green cotton vests, two pairs of Lisle stockings, two pairs of sturdy brown shoes, three shirts that were rough enough to make us itch all the time, ties, and a terrible skirt. None of us were asked what size we were; the clothes were just handed out like potatoes sacks and fitted about as well.

A girl called Mavis tried on the skirt and it immediately fell to the ground. Someone else couldn't get hers over her hips. 'Here, have mine,' Mavis said, holding her skirt out to swap, but they were all the same size so it didn't work. We laughed all the time, but the biggest laugh was the knickers; khaki with legs that came to our knees with elastic round the bottom.

'They're passion-killers if I ever saw anything,' Mavis said, putting a pair on her head and dancing round the room, elasticated legs flying around like floppy dog ears.

'Who needs passion?' Bronwyn muttered.

Next we were handed an ugly tunic. 'Cor, this is bloody awful,' Mavis hooted, 'no one'd know we had knockers wearing this!'

I wasn't used to such talk and I was a bit shocked, but Mavis was so lovely it was impossible to take offence. The tunic was straight up and down with a pretend belt but no belt buckle. Silly. We got a shiny ATS badge, a khaki cap, and a quite nice khaki raincoat. To my surprise we also got a knife, fork, spoon and a tin mug. 'Make sure you wash them after every meal, and bring them with you every time you go to the canteen,' the quartermaster said. Finally, we got a kitbag to put it all in.

Amanda was touching the fabric of the skirt and jacket as if it was something sent down by the devil. I was used to jumble sale clothes converted to fit, so wasn't too upset. Bronwyn though, seemed happy.

'There's lovely,' she said, holding the garments against her, 'never had so many new things in my life.'

We went off to the canteen and all sat together on a long table. An ATS woman came over with two big trays of food. We struck lucky – it was sausage and mash. Mavis leaned over to the next table where a bunch of soldiers were eating. 'Hey,' she complained, 'how come they get more than us?'

The server shrugged her shoulders. 'Men get more,' she said and headed back to the kitchen.

'That ain't fair,' Mavis grumbled.

'I'm going to miss my mum's cooking,' I said as we sat down on the long tables. Our eating irons, as we had to call them, clattered loudly and the noise of about a hundred and fifty people eating and chatting was deafening.

Mavis spat out some greens. 'Wish it was my mum's cooking, too. She never made me eat greens. Nasty things!' She turned to Amanda. 'Your family have a cook, I suppose?'

Amanda blushed again. 'I'm afraid we do. Her name is Betty. I spent a lot of time in the kitchen with her when I was younger. My parents only believed in seeing their children at teatime for about an hour.'

'Blimey, you must hardly know them.' Mavis said, her eyes wide.

Amanda looked down, her hands resting on the table. 'That's true, but Betty was always so friendly and kind. You'll be surprised to know I'm not a bad cook. She used to teach me when I escaped from my nanny.'

I thought how different we four were. Me, with a loving mum. We were poor but never so poor we were hungry. Bronwyn sounded like she'd been hungry a lot of the time and had a lot to put up with. Mavis's family were poor too, but they sounded a good laugh. And Amanda, well, Amanda's family were something else altogether.

No one moaned about lights out at ten, and a lot of girls were asleep even before then. As soon as the lights were off, we took down the blackout blinds to get a bit of fresh air.

I was exhausted from the day, which had been so different from anything else I'd ever experienced. The emotion of getting engaged; leaving Edward; meeting Bronwyn, Mavis and Amanda; and finding my way round this strange new place had taken its toll. I longed for sleep. But when I sat on the mattress I got a nasty surprise.

'Blinking heck,' I said, 'this mattress is made of straw!'

'And the pillow is made of rock,' someone called back.

I took out the picture of Edward, kissed it and put my engagement ring on my finger for the night. Although I was exhausted, it took me a long time to get to sleep, I kept thinking about Edward and hoping he was safe. We'd had so little time together and I didn't even know where he was posted. We could be sent to the other ends of the earth for all I knew. My thoughts were interrupted by someone a few beds down quietly weeping. I crept out of bed and went to her.

'Missing home?' I asked. 'I am. I've never been away before.'

She gave me a wan smile then, without a word, buried her head in her pillow. I took the hint and went back to my bed where the rhythm of Mavis's gentle snores helped me drift off to sleep.

* * *

Next day we were woken at six o'clock. For a minute when I forced my eyes open I couldn't think where I was. No familiar box room; no Mum opening the curtains for me. The noise of the others clattering about the hut soon snapped me back to reality. Several rushed off to the ablutions clutching their dressing gowns round themselves; others got dressed as quickly as possible trying not to show their all to the room. They wriggled out of their pyjama bottoms and into their passion-killers while still under the covers, then tried to hide as they dressed their top half. It was like trying to change into your swimming costume at the beach, only protected by a small towel. I tried not to look, but of course I saw some of it, and it would have been funny if we weren't so cold. I wondered how bad the hut would feel in midwinter and I was grateful to know we would be moved on by then.

Our first job was to clean the hut, even though it seemed perfectly clean. We scrubbed the floors, polished the windows and dusted the metal bits of the bed until the whole place shone. Only then were we allowed to go to breakfast.

'We've got a lecture next,' I said as we sat down with our porridge and tea.

'Cor, what about?' Mavis wanted to know. So did we all.

We soon found out. It was how to recognise an officer, who to salute to and how to salute. We had to stand there in row saluting again and again until the sergeant was happy we'd got it right. Then we learned how to recognise the different bugle calls, from Reveille to Last Post. We'd soon find that the most popular bugle call was the one letting us know the mail had arrived. Finally, we had a general knowledge quiz. I was convinced I'd done badly at that one. 'Right, you lot,' the sergeant said when we'd finished. 'Just time for an hour's square-bashing before you eat. Meet outside in twenty minutes.'

'Whatever's that?' asked Amanda.

Mavis was sitting next to her and nudged her in the ribs. 'You come from a different world, you do. It's learning to march in step – like we saw yesterday when we was coming in the lorry.'

A blush crept up Amanda's neck. 'I've got a lot to learn. You'll have to bear with me. You girls have got more experience of life than me.'

'Not all of it good,' Bronwyn said, her mouth downturned, 'think yourself lucky.'

Amanda smiled at her. 'I know I've been lucky, although being expected to marry the man your parents choose isn't fun. One of the reasons I joined up was to avoid being married off to Sextus – the biggest, stupidest man I have ever known.'

Mavis's jaw dropped. 'Cor, I can marry whoever I like as long as he's not a crim, an' even that's a possibility as long as he's not violent. Why'd they want you to marry such a prat?'

'Money. You'd never believe it was 1940. Some families still expect the gel – that's what they call us, gels, not girls, ladies or women – they expect us gels to marry some rich man who can bolster her family's coffers.'

'What's in it for him, then?' I asked.

'His people wanted him to marry into a titled family; it makes them look good. My mother was all ready to arrange the wedding.

She wanted a big county affair. I had a lucky escape. Sextus and his parents will never forgive me.'

'How did you persuade your parents to let you sign up, then?'

'I didn't. I knew they'd never agree. Women in our family never do any sort of work, much less join the army. I told Mummy I was playing tennis with friends and sneaked off to the recruiting office. I can be very determined if I need to be.'

Mavis gave her a little hug. 'Blimey, who'd've thought I'd one day be sitting next to a swanky girl like you and chatting like we were friends.'

Amanda squeezed her hand. 'We are friends, Mavis. You too, Lily, and you, Bronwyn.' She leaned over to be closer to Bronwyn and spoke quietly. 'Have you noticed those girls over there keep avoiding us? Wherever we sit, they go somewhere else. Is it because of my title, do you think?'

Bronwyn laughed, 'Amanda, *cariad*, I love you dearly, but it's not about you. It's because of me.'

Amanda put her hands over her heart. 'No, surely not, why ever would they?'

I guessed what Bronwyn was going to say. Earlier, when we were cleaning, I was near the other clique and I heard them say things like 'darkie' and 'half-breed' and giving Bronwyn dirty looks.

'It's because of my colour, Amanda,' Bronwyn was saying, 'they hate me because of my colour.'

Amanda's hands went to her face. 'But that's silly. You didn't choose your colour. Now Sextus – he's chosen to eat too much and get fat as a pig and to stay stupid.' She puffed up her cheeks and lolled out her tongue. The combination of her educated voice and silly face had us all in giggles – she had broken the moment. 'Let's stick together, us four,' I said, 'all for one and one for all. If them girls, or anyone else tried to get funny with any of us, we'll take care of it.'

I put my hand in the middle of our little group and everyone put their hand on top of mine.

'It's a deal,' Bronwyn said, giving me a wide smile. 'Come on, time for square-bashing.'

Square-bashing would have been a lot easier if I knew my left from my right. I kept turning the wrong way and earning sniggers from everyone else. After the second time, I got snarled at by Sergeant Terry too. He was a big man with a huge moustache and a nasty attitude. He couldn't have made it clearer that he didn't think women should be in the army.

'Now, Volunteer Baker, what hand do you wear a wedding ring on? Not already married are you?' he said with a sneer.

I straightened my back and looked him in the eye. 'Not married, but I got engaged two days ago.' I instinctively held out my left hand. There was no ring on it. We weren't allowed to wear them on duty, so it was with my things in the hut.

'Volunteer Baker, whatever makes you think I'm interested in your love life?' he shouted. 'Just remember that's your left hand and you'll stop wasting so much valuable army time.'

It worked. I never marched off in the opposite direction to everyone else again.

After our dinner, or lunch as Amanda called it, we were handed buckets, scrubbing brushes and mops.

'Right, you so-called soldiers,' the sergeant said, 'as of now you don't walk anywhere – you march. And that's whether you're on your own or in a group. Hear me? You march. And you don't talk when you're marching.' He paused to make sure we'd heard. 'Anyone heard talking when you march does twenty press-ups. Got it?'

We all nodded, wondering if we'd made a terrible mistake signing up.

'So you've all got it? Now march off to the latrines and make them shine!'

Amanda, who'd been doing a brave job of not complaining about anything, stopped short in the door of the latrines. Her nose wrinkled. 'Ugh, it stinks. What a horrible thing to have to do.'

Bronwyn laughed. 'Think yourself lucky. Where I live there's one toilet for twenty families. It's in a wooden, spider-infested little shed. I'd rather have this luxury any day, even if I do have to clean it now and then.'

'Sorry,' Amanda murmured, picking up her mop she headed for one of the three toilets.

The job didn't take long between the lot of us – the whole bunkhouse full. We were almost finished and most girls had left the room when Dorothy, one of the girls who was rude about Bronwyn, walked past us. Without a glance our way she pretended to trip and split filthy water all over Bronwyn's shoes, muttering 'Monkey' under her breath.

'Oy,' I shouted grabbing her arm, 'apologise! You did that on purpose.'

'Oh yes?' she said with a sneer. 'Prove it!' And with that she turned and stuck her tongue out at Bronwyn. As she turned back, I held out my foot and she went flying, getting some of the dirty water on her uniform.

She stood up and glared at me. 'You did that on purpose!' she hissed.

'Oh yes?' I said, mimicking her tone. 'Prove it!'

When she'd gone, I took out my hankie and handed it to Bronwyn so she could dry her shoes a bit. 'Bronwyn, I'm so sorry that happened to you. What a horrible person she is.'

Bronwyn's shoulders and back looked tense enough to be made

of wood. Her mouth was a tight straight line and her eyes narrowed. 'When you're my colour you get used to things like that.'

'That doesn't make it right,' I said. I tried to give her a hug but she was too rigid.

'No, it blinking well doesn't. We'll have to watch out for that Dorothy and those cronies of hers,' she said.

We soon got into a routine of cleaning, square-bashing, PT, eating and sleeping. But the fifth day was something different.

Sergeant Terry called us to line up immediately after breakfast. 'Right you lot, today you'll be tested to see what jobs you'll be sent to when your training is finished. Get yourself over to G Block now. Quick march!'

My stomach did a flip. I wasn't so scared about the tests because I'd done some exams not long before, but I worried I'd be given some horrible posting and be separated from my new friends.

'What do we get tested on?' Mavis wanted to know. 'I never did very well at tests at school.'

Amanda smiled at her. 'It's nothing like school. We'll get tested on all sorts of things. Things like how to solve mechanical problems...'

Mavis sighed with relief. 'I'll be okay at that, I used to help my brother fix cars.'

'Then we get recognising shapes, spelling, written communication...'

Mavis groaned. 'That's me out then, I'm hopeless at writing letters. Always got terrible marks for English at school.'

'What about maths?' Amanda asked her.

'Well, I can do money and I'm a whiz at doing the score at darts. Does that count?'

There was a fair bit of waiting about as we went in and out of different test rooms. I got to sit with Bronwyn for a while. 'Get your shoes dried okay?' I asked. She just gave a little shrug. 'Just as well they gave us two pairs,' she said. 'I've stuffed newspaper in the wet ones. Mind you, both pairs give me blisters.' She took a shoe off and rubbed her heel. 'Lily, you never told me what you did before you signed up. I worked in a factory.'

'Me too,' I said, 'I sewed buttons on men's shirts, and two evenings a week I was usherette at the Dream Palace. But I went to evening classes and learned how to type and passed the Pitman's exams in English and typing.'

Bronwyn struggled to get her shoe back on. 'What, did you get an office job then?'

'I got really lucky. The manager at the Dream Palace wanted to work a bit less and asked me to be his assistant. I loved it and I got to work with my best friend Jean.'

I paused for a minute. 'Bronwyn, can I ask you a favour?'

'What's that then?' she asked.

'Would you teach me French? You speak it and Amanda said she can speak schoolgirl French. If I can learn it and we're lucky enough to get telephonists posts, we could go to Paris together. Of course, they may not let us, but we might be lucky and I like learning new things.'

'Me? Teach you French?' she said. 'You know I speak it with a West Indian accent?'

'Does that matter? Can people understand you?' I asked.

'I suppose they can,' she said. 'Okay, it'll give us something to do when we're not cleaning latrines. Want to know the word for toilet?'

I grinned at her.

'It's *toilette*. See! Easy-peasy.'

That was the beginning of my French lessons. I soon wished all the words were as easy as that one.

The aptitude tests that day were a real mixture. We were tested on aircraft recognition, hearing, fitness and nerves. 'Can we ask for the job we want?' I asked the tester.

She carried on with her writing. 'You can, but it doesn't mean you'll get it,' she said.

At tea that evening, I asked the others what jobs they wanted to do. About a third wanted to be ack-ack girls helping to man the guns, some wanted to be drivers, three wanted to be motorbike messengers, two wanted to be cooks, two wanted to be orderlies and me, Amanda, Bronwyn and Mavis all put down to be telephonists. Mavis liked the idea of learning French too, so Bronwyn and Amanda taught us every spare minute. We had the names of things in our bit of the hut labelled with their French names and sometimes, when they felt mean, Amanda and Bronwyn only spoke to us in French and we had to guess what they were saying.

Most of us in the bunkhouse spent the last half-hour or so before lights out writing letters to our family and friends or reading letters we'd received. My mum wrote a couple of times in the first week.

Dear Lily,

I hope you are settling in well there and that they are feeding you properly. The house seems very empty without you. After all these years of three of us, your dad leaves and then you, so I've only myself to please. It seems very strange, but I suppose I'll get used to it.

I'm getting used to work at the Filling Factory too. You have to be ever so careful because filling the bombs with explosives is so dangerous. You have to concentrate the whole time and it gets very tiring. But it was tiring being a char, although that was my body that got tired, this is more my mind. But I've already made some good friends there and we're going to the flicks tomorrow so that's something to look forward to.

You know I told you that a man at work kept asking me out? Well, I went for a drink with him a couple of evenings ago. Alex, his name is, and we got on really well, found lots of things to talk about. If I'm still meeting up with him when you get your weekend leave perhaps you could meet him. I'd like to know what you think of him. Isn't that funny, a mum asking her daughter for approval about a man, it should be the other way round! But you've got your lovely Edward. I hope he's keeping safe and writing to you often.

I'm really looking forward to the end of your training so you can come home for your weekend leave.

Love, Mum x

I read and reread her letter so often, it was in danger of falling apart. I hadn't heard from Edward yet and guessed that must mean he was abroad somewhere. Each night I prayed that he was safe from harm.

* * *

Getting ready for bed a few nights later, I sat in my striped pyjamas and reached in my cupboard for my photo of Edward and my ring. I found the photo straight away, but couldn't find the ring. Telling myself not to panic, I took everything out of the cupboard, shook everything and then put them back in. Wondering if I'd absent-mindedly put it in my soap bag I looked there, but no luck.

'What's up?' Bronwyn said from her bed.

'I can't find my engagement ring!' I said, my voice several pitches higher than usual.

'Let me help,' she said and we went through everything together.

It had gone.

2

THE RING

'Someone must have stolen it. It's my fault for showing it off.' My heart sank. That ring had belonged to Edward's grandmother and had special meaning for him as well as me. How would I tell him it was missing? I'd been writing to him regularly but only had one letter back so far. I couldn't imagine writing to him with this news.

Just then the bugle played for lights out. 'We'll hunt again in the morning and think what to do then,' Bronwyn said. 'Chin up. We'll find it.'

If she knew where we would find it, she wouldn't have slept so well that night.

I hardly slept a wink worrying about it. Shivering in the early morning chill, I got up before everyone else to quietly search under my bed, in the covers and under the mattress, as though it would have somehow hidden itself there. There was no sign of it.

Straight after roll call, I went to speak to the section leader and explained what had happened. As I stood there I felt sure I must have made a mistake and I felt sweat dripping down my back. 'Perhaps I've made a mistake,' I said.

'We'll see. We take a very dim view of thieving here,' she said, 'the ATS is no place for thieves. Are you sure you haven't just mislaid it?'

The tears in my eyes were all the answer she needed. 'I'll deal with it,' she said and called all the girls to attention.

'I want all of you back in the bunkhouse. Now!'

We all marched back in – the others confused about what was happening.

'Attention!' Miss Johnson shouted. 'Volunteer Baker has lost her engagement ring. Has anyone seen it?'

No one moved or said a word.

She put her hands on her hips. 'In that case, we may have to assume that someone has stolen it. It's a valuable ring, but more importantly has great sentimental value. I want every one of you to empty your lockers and bags and put everything on your beds now. No exceptions.'

As people walked over to their beds, I pointed out that Julia, who slept at the far end of the bunkhouse, was missing. 'She's been poorly for a couple of days and went to the infirmary last night,' I said.

Section Leader nodded. 'I'll speak to her later,' she said. 'Now empty out your belongings too, so they can see you haven't just mislaid your ring.'

By now there was a good deal of rustling and quiet grumbling as the girls spread their clothes and other things on their blankets.

Section Leader started with the bed nearest mine, the other side from Bronwyn. She got two beds away when Bronwyn suddenly called out, 'It's here!' with a trembling voice. Section Leader walked back and stood by Bronwyn's bed. There, next to her soap bag, was my ring, half wrapped in notepaper. 'I swear I didn't take it!' she said.

'Is this your ring?' Section Leader asked me, holding it up.

I nodded. 'But Bronwyn would never steal it. I'd trust her with my life.'

'You! You! Come with me,' she said indicating me and Bronwyn. She marched out the door with the ring in her hand and we had no choice but to march after her.

She marched us to an office we'd never been in before. 'Sit!' she ordered. 'Now, Volunteer Roberts, how do you explain this ring being in your possession?'

'I can't. I didn't take it. Someone must have put it there,' Bronwyn said, a tear dampening her cheek. 'You won't throw me out, will you? I love the ATS.'

Section Leader took a deep breath. 'I never believe in jumping to conclusions and want to investigate this further. If you didn't take this, who would or could have planted it in with your belongings?'

Bronwyn's eyes slid to mine, but she bit her lip. I know you're not supposed to tell tales but I wasn't going to let Bronwyn take the blame for something she didn't do. 'Three girls have been unkind to Bronwyn because of her skin colour,' I said. 'I don't know if it's anything to do with them.'

'What do you mean unkind?'

'Saying horrible things, calling her names, and two days ago one of them deliberately spilled dirty water on Bronwyn's shoes in the latrine.'

She instinctively looked at Bronwyn's shoes that were as shiny as the day she got them. 'Hmm, that behaviour is one thing, taking a ring is another. Do you have any proof?' she asked.

But of course we didn't.

We gave Miss Johnson the girls' names, but without evidence there was nothing else to do. I was selfish enough to be very glad I had my ring back, but desperately worried about Bronwyn. I just knew she wouldn't have done such a thing.

'Leave this with me until the morning,' Miss Johnson said. 'Meanwhile, carry on with your duties as normal.'

We went to breakfast, the four of us huddling together over our porridge. I kept glancing at Dorothy and her friends. They had their heads close together, giggling and laughing at Bronwyn. Eventually, I could stand it no longer and went over to them.

'Did you steal my ring and plant it in Bronwyn's stuff?' I asked.

Dorothy looked at me as if butter wouldn't melt in her mouth. 'What me?' she said, her hand on her chest. 'I would never do such a thing. I wonder why you'd believe a darkie rather than one of your own?'

Her friends sniggered until I turned on them, pointing. 'You two – you two – you'd better take care.'

'Or else what?' Dorothy said with scorn in her voice.

'Or else next time you trip up it won't be on a nice clean floor.' I had no idea if I'd ever have the nerve to do anything aggressive to her, and they laughed at my words. But I felt better having stood up to her.

The day seemed endless; cleaning, marching, cleaning, marching, and PT. We were getting fitter day by day, but were still very glad when it was time to stop. The four of us walked to the village pub in the evening to avoid Dorothy. It was unusually quiet.

'I heard one lot shipped out this afternoon,' Mavis said, 'another lot'll be here tomorrow drowning their sorrows and wondering what's hit them.'

We played dominoes and darts and tried to keep our spirits up, but we all knew we were just play-acting. We gloomily drank our half-pints of stout and left after an hour, with few words shared between us. When we went back in the bunkhouse we stood around the stove trying to warm our hands. Dorothy shouted from her bed, 'Hide all your stuff girls, thief in the room!'

Mavis put her hands on her hips and shouted back. 'Shut your cakehole, you rotter!'

Amanda, bless her, calmly walked over to Dorothy and stood next to her speaking quietly. I don't know what she said, and she wouldn't tell us, but Dorothy didn't say another word that evening.

Amanda, Mavis and I all went to sit with Bronwyn until lights out. We wondered what the future would hold for her.

My dreams were full of Edward and my missing ring and I must have woken up with the scratchy sheets wrapped round me half a dozen times. Eventually, an hour earlier than necessary, I gave up trying to sleep and quietly got dressed. Bronwyn stirred and I apologised for disturbing her.

'Didn't sleep very well either,' she whispered. 'Hang on, I'll come with you. We can go for a walk.'

The morning was cool and hazy and we were glad of our khaki raincoats. The ghost-grey mist settled like tiny diamonds on our hair, and threw mirage-like shapes as it moved with the breeze. My nose twitched as cooking smells drifted from the canteen and tugged at us, tempting us to turn back immediately. I looked at my watch; too early for them to be serving breakfast.

Bronwyn had dark rings round her eyes that matched mine. 'Do you think they'll throw me out?' she said, a quiver in her voice. 'I don't want to go back home. It's horrible there; I never want to live like that again.'

I touched her arm. 'Bronwyn, whatever happens, I know you didn't take my ring. You're one of the good ones. Let's hope they find the real culprit.'

She gave a weak smile. 'Well, at least they can't court-martial me. We're not part of the army yet.'

'I'm so sorry you're having to go through this. Is it so awful in Swansea?'

She pulled a face. 'My ma's okay and the kids too, although

there's too many for the rooms we rent. Never a halfpenny to spare, bread and jam for meals if we're lucky. Ma's latest bloke is what I'm most desperate to get away from. A bit too handy, if you know what I mean.'

I frowned. 'You mean he hits you?'

She stopped in her tracks. 'Lily, you've no idea how lucky you are. No, that's not how he's handy.'

But she wouldn't explain further.

After a couple of minutes walking in silence, she said, 'Tell me about how your Edward proposed. It'll take my mind off what's coming if they don't find who stole your ring.'

We took the road out of the camp, already busy with army trucks and cars going in and out. Soldiers wolf-whistled and shouted, 'Morning, darling,' as they drove past. We waved to them and veered off the road and along a path through a barren field. The mist was already clearing and it promised to be a lovely winter day.

'It was in the café in the railway station,' I said. 'What was?'

Bronwyn asked, her mind already elsewhere. She had a lot to worry about. I felt desperately sorry for her. To have all she'd worked for taken away for something that wasn't her fault.

'You asked me about how Edward proposed.'

'Oh yes, go on. I could do with hearing something nice, like.' She linked her arm through mine and we matched steps as we walked.

'It was in the café in the railway station the day I left to come here – just before I met you on that train. Remember? We're not a bit alike, did I tell you that? He comes from a professional family and mine aren't at all posh. His mum must be furious 'cos she wanted to pick his wife.'

'Let me guess,' she said, 'someone like Amanda.'

'Exactly. They'd have been a good match, although Amanda's

family are even grander than his. Anyway, I was coming here and he was off to his next posting so we only had about three-quarters of an hour together that day. I never thought in a million years he'd want to marry me.'

She squeezed my elbow. 'There's lovely. Just goes to show he's got good taste. Did he get down on one knee right there in the café?'

'He did, and nearly flattened a little dog who'd been minding his own business sniffing round our feet.'

She kicked up some leaves and they danced in the air. 'So you said yes right away, I'll bet.'

'I hesitated for a minute. I've always been worried about the differences between us. But do you know, by now everyone in the café was listening to us. You could've heard a pin drop. Then the Tannoy announced a train coming and someone shouted, "Hurry up and make up your mind, love, we've got a train to catch!"'

'He didn't!' she laughed.

'He did, and they all clapped and cheered when I said yes.'

She turned and gave me a hug. 'There's a story to tell your grandchildren. I hope I get to meet your Edward one day.'

'So do I,' I said, suddenly serious. 'We've all just got to stay alive until the end of this war.'

I looked at my watch, 'We'd better get back or we won't get any of that bacon.'

* * *

We finished our breakfast and washed our eating irons. As we were leaving, Miss Johnson stopped me and Bronwyn. 'The office. Now,' she said, and moved further along the table.

As we walked, fear made our steps clumsy. 'I'm not being

funny, but I think I've had my chips,' Bronwyn said. 'Might as well pack up and go back home now.'

We were halfway across the parade ground when I glanced back and saw Dorothy was trailing behind Miss Johnson. I nudged Bronwyn. 'Keep marching, don't look round, but I think Dorothy is in on whatever's going to happen next.'

Bronwyn let out a low whistle and her marching became a bit more upright and determined.

In the office, Miss Johnson made us and Dorothy stand to attention in front of her desk while she sat down.

'Now, let's get some rules before we start,' she said. 'I will invite each of you to speak when I want you to. There will be no inter-rupting, no arguments. Understand?'

We chorused, 'Yes, Miss Johnson.'

'Right,' she said, 'you discovered your ring was missing two evenings ago. Is that correct, Volunteer Baker?'

'Yes, miss.' My mouth was so dry words wouldn't come.

'Volunteer Roberts, the ring was found in your bag. Is that correct?'

Bronwyn's face crumpled and she nodded agreement. 'Yes, miss, but I didn't take it.'

Miss was very serious. 'We'll see about that,' she said. 'Now, Volunteer Thomson, I understand you have accused Volunteer Roberts of stealing the ring. Is that correct?'

Dorothy's face could have given a beetroot a run for its money. 'Well... I... I was just joking,' she spluttered, 'but it was in her bag.'

'I have spoken to other people in your hut and some of them tell me that your accusation sounded very serious. Did you see Volunteer Roberts take the ring?'

There was a long pause and Dorothy's red face went paler than pale. I thought she was going to faint. 'No... I... I didn't see her, but the ring was in her bag like you saw.'

Miss stood up. 'So you're telling me, Volunteer Thomson, that you had nothing to do with the theft of this ring. Is that correct?'

Dorothy managed to pull an outraged face and she put her hands on her hips. 'Are you accusing me? Me?' Her voice rose to a screech.

'Volunteer Thomson, I'd like to remind you who you're speaking to. Stand to attention. Now!'

Dorothy snapped her heels together, her arms still by her side, her face a rigid mask.

'Wait here for me,' Miss Johnson said, 'and not a word from any of you. I'll know.'

She marched out of the door and we stood like statues, not daring to move or speak. Two minutes later she was back with Julia, the girl who'd been poorly. She looked very washed out and wearing pyjamas under her raincoat.

'Sit down, Volunteer Smith,' Miss said, holding out a chair for her. 'And thank you again for getting out of your sickbed.'

Julia's face was sickly white and her usually wavy hair was lank and greasy. She was always a tiny stick of a thing, but even thinner than two days ago. 'It's okay,' she said, so quietly we had trouble hearing her.

Miss looked at the three of us standing to attention. 'I was able to speak to Volunteer Smith and she had an interesting tale to tell. Do you feel up to repeating it?' she asked Julia.

Julia nodded. She looked at me and Bronwyn, but I noticed she avoided looking at Dorothy. 'I've been poorly for a few days and two days ago I was in bed when everyone else was out of the hut. I'd been sleeping, but something woke me. I was feeling groggy and didn't move.'

'What did you see, Volunteer Smith?' Miss asked. Julia went even paler. 'I saw... I saw... Dorothy... Volunteer Thomson. She must have thought I was still asleep. She had taken off her shoes and was tiptoeing round the hut.'

I glanced at Dorothy. Her face was unmoving.

'You must have been hallucinating,' she said through gritted teeth.

'Speak when asked to, Volunteer Thomson,' Miss said, 'I won't tell you again.'

Julia finally turned to Dorothy. 'No, I wasn't hallucinating. I saw you as clear as I see you now.'

She turned back to Miss. 'Dorothy... Volunteer Thomson... went to Lily's locker and took something out. I couldn't see what it was but it was small enough to hold in her hand. Then she went to Bronwyn's locker and put whatever it was in there.'

She slumped back in the chair as if the effort of saying all that had been too much.

Miss put her hand lightly on Julia's shoulder. 'Volunteer Smith, thank you for telling us about that. Can I escort you back to the sick bay? You must want to get back in your warm bed.'

Julia struggled to her feet. 'That's okay, I'll manage, thank you, it's not far.'

We waited silently until she'd left. Then Miss spoke. 'What have you got to say for yourself, Volunteer Thomson?'

Dorothy was silent for a minute. Then, 'Well, she was ill, she obviously imagined it.' She turned to look at Bronwyn. 'Everyone knows you can't trust these half-breeds.' As she spoke, her tone became more sneering and her top lip curled.

Miss spoke. 'Volunteer Thomson, I think you would be wise to stop speaking now. If it was within my power to court-martial you, I would do so.'

I heard a sharp intake of breath from Dorothy. 'But as I am unable to do that you will be moved permanently to a different hut immediately and will be on latrine duty for the next month. We do not take lying and stealing lightly in the ATS.'

She turned to me and Bronwyn. 'Now you two may go. Thomson, wait here, I have other things to say to you.'

Next morning, I was woken up to a hubbub in the hut. 'She's gone,' one of Dorothy's friends was saying. 'I went for a walk and put my head round her new hut, but there was no sign of her.'

It was not an offence to desert the ATS. Sometimes girls left because they couldn't stand the army life. Others left because they were in trouble of some sort. Maybe Dorothy didn't want the embarrassment of being found out, or perhaps a month of latrine duty was too much to bear. Whatever the reason, Dorothy and all her belongings had vanished.

3

CELEBRATING

That evening we decided to celebrate Bronwyn being found innocent by going to the dance in town. We could get in half price if we wore uniform, so we made sure we were extra smart as we got ready.

'Do you think it's okay for me to go to a dance when I'm engaged to Edward?' I asked Mavis.

Her jaw dropped. 'Why ever not? You're not going to find yourself another man and go up against a wall with him, are you.'

I frowned. 'What do you mean, go up against a wall?'

'Oh, come on, I know you're an innocent but you must know.' She raised an eyebrow.

I shook my head.

She gave a little laugh. 'It means doing it. You know, doing it.'

'Oh, I never...' I wished I'd never asked.

'What? You never done it? Round our way, if you ain't done it by the time you're sixteen you start to wonder if there's something wrong with you. Your Edward never tried it on?'

I shook my head silently, I'd never had such intimate conversations with anyone before and felt awkward and silly. Making an excuse, I picked up my things and left the latrines, wondering if there was something wrong with me that Edward hadn't pushed for us to go all the way.

Mavis and me were friends again as soon as we got back to the others, and set off to the dance in high spirits.

It was a freezing evening. Stars freckled the sky, and tree branches looked like giant's arms against the dark navy sky – mysterious, powerful. We heard owls, and squirrels scurrying along the grass and up trees. The smell of winter, damp and heavy, surrounded us. The dance hall was packed, mostly with men and women in uniform, all taking advantage of half-price entry. Some sat quietly drinking, others stood flirting but most were dancing like they might be dead soon.

Perhaps some would.

'Let's have port and lemons,' Amanda said when we'd taken off our coats, 'or gin and tonic. My parents have that every night before dinner.'

I'd only ever drunk cider or stout but decided to try the port and lemon. At first I didn't think I liked it, but after the third sip I changed my mind and looked forward to the next one immediately. So I had a second, and a third, just to keep up with the others. After three, Mavis was the only one not a bit tipsy. 'You lot woozy on three port and lemons? You need more practice.' She laughed. 'Come on, let's dance.'

As she spoke a soldier came up and asked her to dance with him. They were soon doing the Lindy Hop.

'I don't know how she can be tossed around like that after all that alcohol and not throw up,' I said.

The rest of us sat nursing our fourth port and lemon, watching her a bit enviously. After three dances, she vanished from sight. The room was crowded and we weren't worried. 'They've probably gone outside for some fresh air,' Amanda said. 'I don't think I'm going to have any more port and lemon. Just lemonade for me from now on. Mummy always used to say that it's easy to make silly decisions when you're a bit tipsy.'

I nodded, half listening, then remembered what Mavis said about being up against a wall, but didn't say anything, telling myself I had an overactive imagination. Fifteen minutes later she was back holding another port and lemon, and wearing a smug smile, her hair slightly untidy.

'Where'd you get to?' Bronwyn asked.

Mavis tapped the side of her nose. 'That's for me to know,' she said with a laugh.

By the end of the evening we'd all been asked to dance several times, although I made sure not to do the slow, smoochy numbers with anyone; that would have felt disloyal to Edward.

We staggered back from the dance singing 'South of the Border' and 'Somewhere in France With You' at the top of our voices. A couple of times, when the path was wide enough, we linked arms and stepped out together like the characters from *The Wizard of Oz*. 'I wonder where the Yellow Brick Road will lead us,' Bronwyn said.

'Paris!' I shouted, my voice a bit slurred.

'Let's hope so,' Mavis said with a giggle, 'I've always wanted to go out with a French man – such a sexy accent.'

I'd never had a hangover before and woke up next morning with my head full of storm clouds that swirled around my skull making me feel sick. My mouth was so dry I had to prise my lips apart and my stomach gurgled loudly. I wasn't even sure I could stand up straight, and when I tried, the room moved as if I were on a ship. It took me a minute to realise I wasn't ill, it was all down to those port and lemons. Bronwyn was struggling to sit upright in her bed next to mine. Her hair was all over the place and she had dark rings round her eyes. 'You look dreadful,' she mumbled, then held her head in her hands. 'Oh, my head. Did we really drink six port and lemons?'

But we knew the ATS wouldn't let us off a day's training for a hangover. 'Come on, get up. If they realise we've got a hangover, they'll probably put us on latrine duty,' I said, clutching on to the bedhead for support. The smell of breakfast made my stomach turn and for the first time, I was grateful it wasn't egg and bacon.

'I wonder if we'll ever get to France,' I said as I ate my porridge more slowly than I'd ever eaten it before.

'Well, you and Mavis haven't done bad learning French. Wouldn't call you fluent yet, though,' Bronwyn said.

'*Vous apprenez vite*,' Amanda said.

I smiled, pleased with myself that I understood. '*Oui, merci*,' I quipped, 'you two are good teachers.'

We washed our eating irons and headed out for yet more square-bashing; this time along the road from the camp. After five minutes I was relieved to find the rhythm and the cool air cleared my head. By now we were a disciplined group, and even my feet did what they were supposed to do. The marching kept the worst of the cold at bay and we sang as we walked, 'Deep in the heart of Texas' and 'Kiss Me Goodnight, Sergeant-Major'. Marching, which we'd hated so much when we first joined up, lifted our spirits that day. And better was to come.

We just returned to the camp when word went round that our postings were on the board outside the office. We'd all put down to be telephonists, but the odds on us staying together were slight even if we got our wish. What if I got an awful posting doing something I hated, somewhere I didn't want to go?

There was a real crowd around the board where postings were listed, girls were groaning or jumping with delight. It took a few minutes to find our names.

When I saw mine, my heart skipped a beat. 'I've got it, telephonist!' I joined the girls who were jumping up and down, a silly grin on my face – jubilant, overjoyed.

The others smiled and nudged me out of the way so they could see their new roles.

'Me, too,' said Amanda, twirling me round, our hats flying off onto the damp ground.

'And me!' That was Bronwyn.

Mavis's face fell. 'Bugger! I'm going to be an orderly. I want to be a telephonist! I want to go to Paris!' she said, her shoulder sagging as if they supported the weight of the world. 'Oh well, might be worse, I suppose. Might've been a cook, then no one would have liked their food ever again. I'll miss you lot though.'

'But we won't know where we're posted for a few more days, Mavis,' I said, 'you might end up with one of us. Let's all pray tonight that we get to stay together.'

I wrote to Edward that night to tell him my good news. I hadn't heard from him for a week and worried that something had happened to him, although everyone kept saying it was just the post being in a muddle.

I read and reread his last letter until it was ready to fall apart.

Dearest Lily,

Every time I get a letter from you, my heart gives a happy leap. I'm very sorry that I haven't written as often as you. Sometimes our work here makes it impossible or I would have done so. I wish I could tell you about it, but you will understand how that is impossible.

I miss you so much, my love, and hope that soon our war work will throw us near each other so we can meet. My next posting is a matter of conjecture, I'm afraid, and I'm guessing that you don't know where you'll be posted yet. Have they told you yet what sort of work you'll be doing? I like the idea of tele-

phonist work, it sounds warm and safe and I do so want you to be safe and well. Let's hope they give you what you want and that your friends can go with you. I have made some good friends here, and when we get a bit of spare time we head to the pub and drown our sorrows.

Keep writing! I miss you. All my love,

Edward

I'd hoped he would be able to get leave for the weekend when my training finished, we'd spent so little time together since we met. I hadn't thought he would get leave at the same time but that didn't stop me feeling down about it. Even though it was just a few short weeks since I'd seen him, it seemed for ever. The other girls and me checked the board every day to see where we were going to be posted. Now that three of us knew we were going to be telephonists, Amanda and Bronwyn got me practising suitable phrases, like 'How can I help you?' in both French and English. Mavis still kept up the lessons too, just in case she got a transfer later. We practised and practised and I managed to get a French language book out of the library and I often studied it for a few minutes after I'd written letters home, or to Edward.

Then the big day came. 'Postings are up!' went the word. We hurried back to the noticeboard outside the office. We couldn't believe our luck, all four of us were being sent to Kensington Training Centre that was just being opened up. Mavis would be an orderly there and the rest of us would learn how to use the switchboards that appeared impossibly complicated from the photos we'd seen. We could not have known the problems that would overcome us there.

* * *

I always said my mum was a mind-reader when it came to me and my movements. The kettle was on and the fire was blazing when I walked through the door, kitbag on my back. She put down the old brown teapot and rushed to give me a hug.

'Lily,' she said, a tear in her eye, 'I've missed you so much. Let me look at you.' She stood back. 'You've lost weight. Didn't they feed you in that camp?'

I put my bag down and took off my coat, 'They did, Mum, but it wasn't up to your standard. It's the square-bashing that's taken off the pounds. It's boring but it makes you fit, I've never felt stronger.'

She hung up my coat and came back into the kitchen.

'Well, come and take the load off your feet and get warm by the fire. Tea's almost ready and there's crumpets to toast.'

We sat down on the brown pretend velvet suite she'd bought, against my dad's wishes, when we first moved to the corporation house from the grotty old slum we'd lived in before. 'Still no word from Dad?' I asked, sitting down in his favourite spot. How good that felt. He'd have been furious if he'd seen me, but now he was banished; a loathsome memory drifting into the past, impotent to wield his vicious power.

She put the tray down, stabbed a crumpet with the long toasting fork and held it in front of the fire. 'No, thank goodness, not a word from him. I hear about him from time to time though. He's still with his fancy woman. Good luck to her, I say, she did me a favour.'

I poured the tea and noticed she'd got the best china out. 'You have to feel sorry for her though. I wonder how long it'll be before he lets his true nature show through. I don't believe he can keep pretending to be nice for long.'

She turned the crumpet over, blowing on her fingers. 'You're not wrong there, Lily. This'll be ready in a minute. Pass your plate. Did you enjoy the training camp? What was it like?'

I passed her tea and a plate. 'The mattresses were made of straw, I'm surprised I'm not two inches shorter from all the square-bashing we did, and we never got a minute to ourselves. But, I did enjoy it, that's what's so weird. I met a lot of new people and learned a lot of interesting stuff.'

She passed me the crumpet. 'Go easy with the marge, love. Not so easy to get now. I'm thinking of having chickens in the garden. Not much room there, but needs must. I'll plant some tomatoes and runner beans come spring, too.'

She sat back and took a bite of her crumpet, closing her eyes briefly as she savoured the taste. 'Mmm, that's good.' She wiped a drip of marge off her chin. 'You know, you going to London and then who-knows-where, doing all this new stuff is really good. No one wants war, but it does give women a chance to do different things, doesn't it? Your life will never be the same and a good thing too. Women my age never expected anything but marriage and kids.'

'But your life's better now Dad's gone, isn't it?' I asked, 'And you've got your new bloke, too.'

She gave a big smile. 'Alex, yes, he's very kind. I hope you'll like him. If you've got time, I said we'd meet him at Woolworths café for a cuppa this afternoon.'

I took a sip of my tea, so much better than the awful stuff at camp. ''Course I will. I'd like to nip and see Jean first though. She's only home for today. Lucky we overlap for a few hours.'

'You must have missed her; you two working together at the shirt factory and the Dream Palace all that time.'

I thought about all the laughs Jean and me had. 'You know I've told you in my letters about the three girls I'm friendly with? Mavis is a lot like Jean. She's a good laugh and a bit too fond of the lads. Heart of gold though. Do you still like working at the Filling Factory?'

She picked up the tea-tray. 'I like the girls I'm working with, but it's dangerous work. You have to concentrate every minute. You can't relax when you're working with explosives. Still, it's better than charring, and the money's good.'

She headed towards the kitchen. 'Off you go, then, and see Jean. I'll have a sandwich and some soup ready when you come back, then we can go into town.'

* * *

Even though Jean was only home for the day, her mum had her looking after her little brother and sister. 'Come on in,' she said when I arrived, 'let's give these little buggers something to eat and drink, then we can bung 'em in the other room so we can chat.'

Like me, she'd lost weight, and the dark rings round her eyes from lack of sleep matched mine.

'Come on, you two,' she said to the kids, handing them the sandwiches and drinks, 'have this and in the other room with you. You've got toys and stuff in there. Let me 'ave ten minutes to talk to Lil. No arguing!'

She wiped their faces and hands with a damp cloth and headed them out of the kitchen. They went off grumbling, their mouths full of jam sandwich.

Jean set about tidying up. 'This place goes to pot if I'm not 'ere,' she muttered. ''Elp me sort it, will ya, then we can sit down. Can't bear to sit in all this clutter.'

I had to laugh. 'Goodness, Jean, the nursing's certainly changed you. I remember when your room was such a mess it was a struggle to get in the door.'

She pulled a face. 'I suppose you're right. Can't have germs in the 'ospital so I suppose it sticks in your brain.' She handed me a tea towel. 'Can you dry that lot?'

'Are you still enjoying nursing?' I asked, drying a plate and putting it on the shelf.

She passed me another one. 'Usually. It feels good to be doing something useful, but sometimes I go to my room at the end of my shift too tired to even clean my teeth.'

'What about lads? Found yourself anyone special?' I picked up the pile of plates and put them in the cupboard.

'There's dozens of lads but most of them are missing something: an arm, a leg, their sight, their brain...'

I turned to face her. 'Oh, Jean, that's so sad. Thank goodness they've got someone like you to help them.'

She turned back to the sink. 'I flirt and joke with them, try to cheer 'em up even though I get in trouble over it from Sister. I reckon they deserve a bit of a laugh with what's 'appened to them. And some of them will never be the same again, poor sods. Can you do these last plates? Then we're done.'

'Is it all soldiers then?' I asked.

She started to wipe the table down. 'We get a few local girls in the women's ward. Some of 'em 'ave got diseases off the soldiers and don't know until they're really ill. Others come in 'cos they've tried to get rid of a baby. 'Orrible it is. I feel so sorry for 'em. Let's talk about something more cheerful. We're both going to be in London while you're doing your training.' She stood up and put the dishcloth over the taps, then dried her hands on her pinny. 'Let's fix up to meet when we're both off duty. We can go to a dance or the flicks or something.'

'Let's hope our shifts work out right. Jean, can I talk to you about something? I'm a bit worried 'cos I haven't heard from Edward for two weeks. D'you think anything's happened to him?'

She hung the tea towel over the mangle. 'You'd 'ave 'eard, wouldn't you? Surely his mum would tell you even if you're not next of kin yet.'

'That's it – I'm not sure she would. She never approved of me – not her sort of person at all. And now I'm in the ATS, she probably thinks I'm on the game or an officer's groundsheet like they say in the papers.' She leaned against the sink and folded her arms.

'Why don't you go round and ask 'er, then?'

My stomach clenched. 'Oh no, I couldn't, it was bad enough meeting her with Edward. I went round once and you wouldn't believe how off she was with me.'

Jean leaned over and squeezed my hand. 'Write 'er a letter then, if you don't 'ear in a few days. But odds are Edward's letter is just in the post, you know what it's like.'

When I left an hour later, I felt blessed to have such a good friend, and grateful for the new friends in the ATS. But I was still worried about Edward.

4

THE RAT

Woolworths café was huge. The rectangular tables were lined up so precisely you'd have thought our sergeant had done them. A long counter with all the dishes was against one wall. There was a fair bit on the menu, and my mouth watered as I read down the list.

Lancashire Meat and Potato Pie 7d
Cottage Pie and Peas 6d
Roast shoulder of lamp and mint sauce 7d
Grilled pork sausages 8d
Steamed fruit roll and custard sauce 3d

After the food at the training camp and all the restrictions with rationing, this seemed like food from heaven and I wished we hadn't already eaten.

Alex was waiting for us, a smile on his face. I tried not to laugh but he was a dead ringer for Arthur Askey, all long face and straight hair.

'Lovely to meet you, Lily,' he said shaking my hand, 'your

mum's told me a lot about you, but she didn't say how pretty you are. Let's join the queue and get some tea and buns, then we can sit down and get to know each other.'

We had to take a tray and join a queue behind a metal bar. Then we shuffled along until it was our turn. Mum went ahead, then me, and then Alex. Once I felt him press against me, but didn't think much of it, I just thought someone had pushed into him. But then a minute later, when Mum was telling the server what she wanted, he squeezed my bottom hard. 'Like that, do you?' he whispered in my ear, his hot breath singeing my neck.

I jumped away from him and nearly knocked Mum over. 'You okay?' she asked. I could hardly breathe, let alone speak and I just nodded, feeling a fool.

Alex glanced over my shoulder and spoke to her. 'Find something you like, love?' he asked. She gave him a smile and turned to pick up her tray.

When he was sure she was looking away, Alex pushed my hair out of the way and whispered in my ear, 'Like the boys, do you? Us mature men know what we're doing a lot more. You should give us a try.' I couldn't believe my ears. My mum's new man trying to get fresh with me and not two foot away from her. I took a deep breath and stepped back heavily on his foot.

'Ouch, that hurt,' he said, hopping up and down, 'like a bit of a fight, do you?' He gave a suggestive grin and raised one eyebrow as if expecting an answer.

Thank goodness we'd got to the pay desk, and he paid for all our tea and cakes, while I edged as far away from him as possible.

We found a table, but I was so shocked at his behaviour I didn't say much as we drank our tea.

'You okay?' Mum asked. 'You're not usually this quiet.'

Alex put his hand over mine. 'I expect it's just meeting someone new,' he said.

I jerked my hand away like it had been burned.

'I feel a bit sick,' I said, pushing my chair back, 'I'm going to go home. You have a nice time and I'll see you later, Mum.'

I didn't want to go home after being bothered by Alex. I knew Mum would fret about me and I needed a bit of thinking time alone. What should I do? Tell her and spoil her budding romance? Would she even believe me if Alex denied it? But if I didn't say anything and the relationship continued, she was at risk of being with someone who would two-time her. I hated the idea of her being treated badly again. She deserved better.

I walked towards my old workplace and the weather matched my mood. The sky was low, with myriad shades of grey and a persistent drizzle making it almost as dark as pre-dawn.

Somehow, I'd expected the Dream Palace to be changed, so was surprised to find it seem exactly the same as six eventful weeks ago. I was disappointed to find my old boss, Mr Simmons, wasn't on duty, but I knew the usherettes and we had a great time catching up on news. They sneaked me in to see a film for free. It was just what I needed, *Haunted Honeymoon* with Robert Montgomery. As I watched the silly things Lord Peter Wimsey got up to, I felt the knots in my forehead and shoulders relaxing.

I decided not to do anything about Alex yet. I'd carry on the weekend as planned. Then if Mum continued seeing him, I'd make a decision what to do. I felt a bit of a coward not telling her, but perhaps they'd stop seeing each other anyway, and I didn't want to be the bearer of bad news.

The weekend leave passed quickly and we didn't see Alex again, thank goodness. I helped Mum make some curtains with material she'd got from the market.

'This beige will go well with the three piece suite,' I said, as we pinned up the hem.

She took a pin out of her mouth. 'Mmm, we'll get these up and then I'll walk you to the station. I meant to ask you, where are you staying in London?'

'You'll never guess. It's a hotel. The Surrey Hotel, not far from the training centre in Kensington. I've never stayed in a hotel before, have you?'

'Two nights on honeymoon with your dad, that's all,' she said. 'It was a bit of a fleapit to be honest. But I'm going to worry about you being there. There's a lot of talk about bombing really getting going soon.'

'I'll be fine, Mum,' I said, and hoped that I spoke the truth.

'Think you'll get home for Christmas?' she asked.

'I wish I knew. We all keep asking but they never give us an answer.' I finished the last bit of hem and got out the iron ready to make them perfect for hanging.

Before we knew it, we were walking back to the station, this time to get the London train.

* * *

16 February 1940

Although no bombs had dropped yet, the war was everywhere on my walk from the underground station to The Surrey Hotel. Men and women in uniform hurried here and there; windows were taped with big crosses; and posters telling us to 'Keep it Under our Hats' and 'Careless Talk Costs Lives' were constant reminders of the danger we all faced. Operation Pied Piper was well underway and there didn't seem many children about, although I did see a group at the station. They carried tiny cardboard suitcases or bags with their belongings and they all had labels with their names on. The women looking after them had a tough job. Some were full of nervous excitement at going somewhere new, some were quietly scared and others sobbed uncontrollably. I wanted to scoop them up and give them a hug. At the same time, parents were bringing their children back because the bombing the government had warned us about hadn't happened.

I shivered with cold as I walked along, noticing a newspaper seller's headline that three hundred prisoners of war had been rescued from a ship in Norwegian waters. I wondered if Edward was amongst them.

I'd only been to London once before, and I'd never been to Kensington. I gazed at the big houses and expensive cars, wondering what it would be like to live the lives these people lived. But I also gaped at some terrible buildings that needed to be condemned. Yet people were still living in them – tattered curtains at the broken windows; rubbish and old broken-down bikes and prams everywhere. Did they look enviously at the rich people every day, or were they too worried about getting enough to eat to think about it?

As I checked I was in the right place, two underdressed kids in the street laughed at me, jumped up and down and scratched under their arms like monkeys. One started inspecting the other one's head as if for nits. I wondered what that was all about. My feet ached and I hoped I someone would make me a cup of tea and maybe bring it to my room.

I was about to get a rude awaking from that daydream.

The Surrey was way past down at heel. Paint flaked from the walls outside and the lettering was hanging at odd angles, ready to fall on the head of any unsuspecting passer-by. Kids had drawn rude pictures on the walls and there was dog business here and there on the pavement outside.

Checking my shoes, I climbed the three steps into the hotel, and looked around the foyer expecting to see a receptionist.

The foyer was empty.

Completely empty. No furniture, no carpets, no reception desk, nothing. I went back outside and checked it was the right place. Yes, the wonky lettering definitely said The Surrey. With a sinking feeling I went back in and noticed the musty smell about the place and the way my footsteps echoed down the corridors. As I stood wondering what to do, another ATS girl in uniform walked in, did a double-take and stood frowning.

'Am I in the right place?' she asked of no one in particular.

'You here for telephonist training, too?'

She nodded. 'Well, I thought I was. What is this place? Ghost hotel? I'm Agnes by the way.'

'Lily. Blimey, I hope the place isn't haunted. Mind you, there certainly doesn't seem to be any sign of life here. We'd better go and see if we can find anyone.' I hitched my kitbag further on my shoulder and we walked along the corridor almost on tiptoe as if to avoid waking the dead. We stopped every few steps to listen. We heard worrying scratching sounds and the dull hum of occasional cars outside, but nothing else. The only light was behind us from the entrance hall and from one window ahead of us. They didn't show us much because light was fading fast and anyway, they were thick with dust.

We almost jumped out of our shoes when a door was suddenly flung open and a voice boomed, 'We'll get this sorted, girls!' A woman emerged who almost walked into us in her haste to leave the building.

'Oh! Girls!' she said stopping in her tracks. 'Welcome. I'm Miss Rounds, your telephone tutor.' The name didn't suit her at all. She was tall, thin and had hair scraped tight in a bun.

'Bit of a problem with the necessary,' she continued. 'I'm going to make some phone calls and I'll be right back.' She pointed to the room she'd just left, 'The others are in there, go and get to know them.'

She marched off down the corridor, her heels beating a tattoo on the wooden floor.

There were three other girls waiting in the room and I was delighted to see Bronwyn was one of them. We grinned and I went and linked arms with her. Only then did I register the room.

'Where's the furniture?' I asked. 'Were they robbed?'

Bronwyn shrugged. 'Search me. Miss Rounds said that the ATS is growing so quickly a lot of things haven't been properly organised yet. Well, she didn't say it like that, but that's what she meant. She's gone off to find us some beds or somewhere else to stay.'

It was getting dark and I clicked the light switch. Nothing happened. 'Is this whole hotel completely empty?'

'Emptier than the *Mary Celeste*,' one of the others said, 'at least that still had some furniture. We haven't even got anywhere to sit.' And with that she sat on the dusty floor. We all followed suit.

An hour later, by which time it was completely dark, Miss Rounds came back. She had a torch and a Tilly lamp. Behind her was a man pulling a trolley.

'Rotten business this, girls,' she said, reaching over to the trolley and pulling off a bundle of blankets. 'No beds and nowhere else to go. We'll have to put up with this place tonight. But I've got blankets and some sandwiches and pop so we'll survive until the morning when we go to our training centre.'

'Isn't this the training centre, then?' Bronwyn asked.

'Goodness me, no, that's down the road a bit. This is supposed to be your accommodation. But buck up, girls, I'm sure we'll have it all sorted out by tomorrow night.'

As she organised blankets and sandwiches, four more girls arrived, including Amanda. 'We're expecting four more,' Miss Rounds said, still maintaining her jolly hockey sticks voice, 'but they will join us in the morning.'

'Miss Rounds, how about if we all go to a pub when we've eaten our sandwiches? I saw one on the corner,' Bronwyn asked. That got a cheer all round, so we folded our blankets for makeshift seats, ate our sandwiches as quickly as possible and headed to the pub where there was light and heat. It turned out the Eagle and Child was barely warmer than the street outside, but it had a log fire and was a welcome sight after the hotel we'd just left. 'If you all have soft drinks, they're on me,' Miss Round said.

'You've got to give her credit for trying,' Amanda said, 'it can't be easy for her making the best of this mess.'

A group of three older men sat near us. They all wore flat caps and were well wrapped up against the cold with winter coats and scarves even though they were indoors.

After we'd been chatting a few minutes, one of them leaned over. 'Did I hear you say you're staying at that old hotel over the road?' he asked. We nodded. 'Well, good luck with that. You'll need it.' Try as we might, he wouldn't be drawn any further about what was wrong with the place.

'Well, I never,' Bronwyn said, 'I wonder if it is haunted – it's got a spooky feel about it.'

'Or maybe it's got dry rot,' one of the others said, 'but can't you smell that?'

* * *

It was a cold and uncomfortable night lying on the floor. I began to remember the horrible straw mattresses in the bunkhouse fondly. We only had one blanket each wrapped tightly round ourselves and a kitbag for a pillow. I woke up shivery and itchy a few times in the night, confused where I was until I saw the sleeping bodies on the floor around me.

Next morning we woke early, stiff and grumpy from a poor night. Then we started to scratch. And scratch. And scratch.

Amanda peered in a mottled mirror on one of the peeling walls and let out a wail, 'I've got measles!' she said, scratching her face which must have had at least ten spots on it. The rest of us started to inspect ourselves. We all had itchy spots. They were everywhere. 'Measles, measles' was repeated again and again until Bronwyn started to laugh.

'Tell you've never lived anywhere rough,' she said. 'We can't all get measles at the same time like that. I'm not going to lie to you, it's like this 'ere. They're not measles spots, they're flea bites!'

There was a moment's stunned silence then the blankets were thrown down as if they held plague germs and we all rushed out of the building as fast as our legs would take us. When we got outside the same boys were there. They grinned and started doing the monkey grooming impersonations again. This time I understood why.

* * *

We rushed round to the public baths where we all scrubbed our skin until we looked sunburnt. I refused to put my uniform on and took my spare from my kitbag, hoping the fleas hadn't got in there too. 'Check the seams,' Bronwyn advised. 'That's where the little buggers'll hide. If you find any, squash them between your finger and thumb.' It took ages, but I finally felt safe to put the uniform on, bundling up the other one in newspaper to get it washed.

Then we went to a café for tea and toast and so the start of our telephone training was very late.

The training room was in a building full of army offices. Miss Rounds hurried us there on that first day, walking us briskly down the corridors without looking left or right. Men and women in uniform walked around importantly, holding folders or piles of paper. They ignored us so completely it was as if we were invisible.

'Come on, girls,' Miss Rounds called over her shoulder, 'all the work here is very hush-hush so don't expect to be socialising with anyone. We keep to ourselves and they do the same. Better for security.'

Our room would have been bright and sunny if there'd been any sun. It was one of those dull, winter days when the clouds seem to be trying to reach the ground and you wish it was summer. It was a corner room with a high ceiling and tall windows on two sides. A bank of telephone equipment took up most of one wall. On the opposite side were some small tables and some hard chairs. We learned they were where we would take our breaks.

'Right, girls.' Miss Rounds said, 'You'll be learning how to operate different types of switchboards, what to say and the right voice to use. But first, go to get your headsets.'

By the end of the first day my head was fit to burst – cords, plugs, flashing lights, enunciation. I wondered if I'd ever get the hang of it all.

We had some good news by late afternoon. Miss Rounds clapped her hands. 'Gather round, girls. We have found an empty school about twenty minutes' walk from here and that will be your new billet. I'm assured there are no infestations and there is electricity and running water.'

'Will we have beds?' someone asked.

Miss Rounds nodded. 'Camp beds for now, I'm afraid, but better than the floor. And you can keep your things in the children's lockers. I've arranged for all the beds to be put in the school hall, easier to heat one room and make sure the blackouts are done properly.'

We headed off to the billet that was to be our new temporary home. It was an intimidating Victorian school, mock Gothic, with high windows you couldn't see out of, and high ceilings too. 'I went to a school like this,' I said. 'I bet they made the windows so high to stop the kids getting distracted by more interesting things than their lessons.'

But we all felt better when we saw the camp beds set up in the echoey hall which was clean even if a bit chilly. The staffroom still had some battered armchairs in it and a tatty coffee table. Miss Rounds had found a kettle for the gas ring and some cups and plates, so we thought we'd manage okay.

Bronwyn came into the room laughing. 'Hope you've got good thigh muscles, girls. This must've been a primary school. The toilets are all tiny; it's like squatting on a guzunder!'

The next night Bronwyn, Amanda and me met up with Mavis, who was now an orderly in a building about a mile from the school we were billeted in. We braved the weather and went to a pub nearby. Two morose old men with flat caps and clay pipes were the only customers, so the barman perked up when we walked in. He was a tall, bald man with a stomach so big you had to wonder how he reached everything in the bar without his stomach knocking glasses and bottles flying.

'You're like a ray of sunshine walking in, girls. What can I get you? Old enough to drink, are you?' He winked as he reached for glasses.

'Flatterer!' Mavis quipped, fluttering her eyelids at him. She got a free drink for her trouble.

We got our shandies and sat as far from the old men as possible. We regaled Mavis with stories of the 'flea-ridden' hotel.

'Cor,' she said, 'I wish I'd seen it. 'Ere, you've still got a couple of spots on your face, 'aven't you, Amanda! I've 'ad a few flea bites in my time, I can tell you.'

I noticed she seemed a bit peaky. 'You okay, Mavis?' I asked. 'You're very pale.'

She gave a smile that wasn't a hundred per cent convincing.

'Just missing you lot, that's all,' she said. 'No one I like as much as you where I'm working now.'

I felt sad seeing the bleak look in her eyes. 'What work are you doing, Mavis, or is it top secret? Don't tell us if you shouldn't.'

She gave a bitter laugh. 'If you think being a dogsbody is secret, you're much mistaken. It's like they don't know what to do with me, so I'm at everyone's beck and call. I wish they'd find me a proper job to do. There's one good thing though, one of the girls is French and she's 'elping me to keep learning. Can't have you lot leaving me behind.'

'We'll never leave you behind, *cariad*,' Bronwyn said, 'you're much too smart for that. Lily is keeping her practice up too. We're going to stop behind for half an hour every day to practise answering in French on the switchboard.'

Mavis smiled her thanks at the compliment. 'As soon as you know where you're going, let me know and I'll try putting in a transfer – see if we can't all get back together. 'Ey, let's go to a dance on Friday. They've got a good band.'

'I don't know,' I said, nudging her, 'you've only been here two days and you already know all the best places.'

She sat back and folded her arms, 'And, girls, I've got us escorts to the dance. There's four soldiers just dying to have a bit of a bop 'ow about it?'

'I can't do that,' I said, 'what about Edward?'

She slapped my arm. 'I'm not asking you to go out with one of them, you daft thing, it'll be a group, we'll 'ave a dance and a laugh.'

Bronwyn shook her head, 'I'm not sure, I don't go out with lads...'

'D'you go out with girls, then?' Mavis said.

Bronwyn gave her a killer stare. 'No, Mavis, I don't. But if these lads are like most of the ones I know they'll think they can buy us a drink and expect something in return. Just saying.'

I remembered what Bronwyn said about her stepfather being too 'handy'. After my experience with Alex, my mum's man, I began to understand what she might mean. No wonder she wasn't too keen on men.

Mavis put her hands in the air in surrender. 'Okay, what about you, Amanda, you fancy a dance?'

'The others will kill me for saying this, but I do. I think we can fight them off if they get a bit fresh.' She turned to me and Bronwyn. 'Come on. One evening. We deserve a bit of entertainment.'

In the end we gave in, but said we wouldn't go with the lads she'd got lined up. We didn't want them having any expectations of us.

* * *

After days of 'Number, please' and putting plugs into the right holes, we were ready for a bit of fun. Like before, wearing uniform meant we got in half price. I hadn't thought of it before, but it meant we all looked equal. In civvies, Amanda oozed money. Her clothes, shoes, everything, shouted expensive. And Mavis and Bronwyn looked poor. I was somewhere in between, thanks to the dressmaking my mum and me did.

The Locano was packed when we arrived. It was much bigger than any dance hall I'd been to before. At one end, red velvet curtains provided a backdrop to the band who were playing 'On the Outside Looking In'. Dozens of lights illuminated the crowd of men and women dancing or drinking, most in uniform. The men in civvies seemed out of place, and I noticed they seemed a bit jealous of the lads in uniform, or maybe they were upset that the girls went for them. It was mostly soldiers, but there was a good sprinkling of sailors and airmen too.

Before we even had chance to buy our drinks, four soldiers came up to chat to us. 'Buy drinks for you, girls? Hate to see girls all alone,' they said.

'No thanks, we're not alone, we're together. Now buzz off.' Mavis was never one to mince her words.

First drinks finished, we split into pairs and were soon dancing. I felt very guilty having a good time when Edward was goodness knows where facing awful dangers. But I had no intention of doing anything with the lad I danced with. I wasn't even sure I liked him; he had a bit of a know-all attitude, like he knew everything and us girls were second-class somehow.

After two Lindy Hop dances straight off I was so hot, I decided to go outside for a minute to cool off. 'I'll come with you,' he said, 'I can have a fag while I'm out there.' I tried to put him off, but he was pushy and I didn't want to seem rude.

It was a mild night for the time of year, but still so cold that I hugged my uniform jacket tightly to myself. The lad, Jack he said his name was, lit up a ciggie and offered me one. I shook my head.

'Do you good,' he said, 'really clears your chest.' He tried again to push one on me but I refused.

'Had lots of boyfriends, have you?' he asked, taking a drag. 'Bet you have. A smasher like you.'

I was beginning to feel uncomfortable.

'You've no right to make any assumptions about me, and anyway, I'm engaged,' I said, showing my ring. 'I'm going in now.'

I started to walk towards the door when he suddenly grabbed me by the collar and pulled me almost off my feet. He dragged me round the corner of the building, heels sliding on the gravel.

It was dark there and no one could see us. I opened my mouth to scream, but he clamped his big, ciggie-smelling hand across my mouth so hard I wanted to gag.

'Keep quiet and you won't get hurt. Understand?' His gritty voice made me go cold with fear.

A million thoughts raced through my head. Did I do something that made him think I was interested in him or easy to get in bed? Should I fight back or would he kill me? Once more, I tried to scream but his hand stopped any sound.

Too quickly for me to react, he removed his hand and pressed my mouth with lips rough as sandpaper. The rotter pushed so hard I felt my teeth hard against my lip. I whimpered, but he just grunted and pushed his entire body against mine. His hand pushed its way up my skirt as his knee tried to force my legs apart. I was glad all the square-bashing meant that my muscles were strong enough to try to resist him. At the same time, I felt his hard thing against my stomach. The smell of sweat, beer and ciggies made me want to gag. His greasy, Brylcreemed hair left a slimy trail on my forehead. I tried to kick him, but I had no room to manoeuvre.

I was so scared I thought I was going to wet myself.

It was like I had two minds – one frozen with fear, while the other desperately tried to work out how to escape. Kicking hadn't worked, so I pushed myself from the wall as hard as possible hoping to thrust him away from me. It had no effect; he was too strong for me. I struggled to breathe, the rough brick wall behind me crushing me. My heart pounded like it wanted to jump out of my chest.

Then a voice shouted, 'Lily, where are you?' It was Bronwyn.

Her call distracted him for a second, and I had my chance. I freed my hands and yanked hard on his ears. He yelped and covered them with his hands. Then I made a fist and, with the side of it, hit him hard in the nose from underneath.

Bone crunched.

He doubled up and I kneed him where it would hurt, and left him gasping for breath. Wiping my mouth, I ran as fast as I could straight into Bronwyn's arms.

'What is it? What's happened?' Bronwyn asked, her arms round me as I sobbed quietly.

'That soldier, the one I was dancing with... he... he... attacked me...'

'Wait here. I'll be there now, in a minute,' she said and guided me into the dance hall doorway. She ran towards the side of the building where I'd been and I was terrified he was still there and would attack her. But she was back in a few seconds.

'He's gone, the bastard,' she said. 'Do you want to go back in? His friends must know who he is.'

I was still shaking too much to think clearly. 'I... I...'

Bronwyn put her arm through mine. 'Would you rather go back to our billets now? I don't suppose his friends would rat on him anyway. But we need to warn the others what happened so they can be on their guard.'

She was like a rock, and I was so grateful that she was there to help me. She stood me just inside the dance hall, near the ticket booth. 'Take care of my friend for a minute,' Bronwyn said, then headed back inside.

The old lady who'd taken our money was sitting knitting a scarf in dreary brown and black stripes.

She looked up. 'You're a bit pale round the gills,' she said, 'you okay? Something happen? Booze and boys don't mix well, that's what I always say.'

A few minutes later, Bronwyn returned with Mavis and Amanda.

'Bronwyn told us what happened. We're coming back with you,

and we won't take no for an answer,' Amanda said, her forehead creased in a worried frown.

I was beginning to feel a bit calmer. After taking a deep breath I said, 'No, don't let it spoil your evening. Bronwyn will come back with me. I'll be okay.'

But lovely friends that they were, they all kept me company, making sure I felt safe.

As soon as we got back, I went to the bathroom and had a strip-down wash and cleaned my teeth three times.

The next day I woke up feeling shaky, but decided to go ahead with the training, rather than take time off sick. All night I'd been restless, my mind playing the attack over and over and I don't suppose I got more than three or four hours' sleep. But lying around all day wouldn't make it go away. Better to keep busy so that my mind was occupied. The telephonist training certainly did that, and we had one lucky thing happen. Usually Bronwyn, Amanda and I practised our French when Miss Rounds had gone, but on this day she forgot something and came back into the room unexpectedly. Hearing us, she asked if we wanted to be posted to France and promised to help us get there. We thanked her formally, but when she left the room we danced around like a load of crazy women.

'France! I can't believe I'm going to France!' I said.

'Don't count your chickens yet,' Bronwyn said, but her smile showed she was as excited as I was.

* * *

A couple of weeks later, I was surprised to find Mavis waiting for me when the training day finished. Her skin was paler than usual and her hair lank. Even her walk was nothing like her usual bouncy self.

'Did I forget we're meeting?' I asked when I saw her.

She pulled my arm. 'Can we go for a walk? I need to talk to you,' she said, her voice husky and quiet.

I grabbed my coat and gloves and followed her out. Finally, the dank weather had given way to pale winter sunshine throughout the day, but by the time we went for a walk it was dark and the temperature had dropped again sharply.

We walked past Scott's, the ladies' shop where I often gazed in the window wishing I was rich enough to own some of their clothes. We stopped and gazed at the dresses and blouses in silence and I wondered when Mavis would get round to telling me what she wanted to say. We walked all the way to the Victoria and Albert Museum before she spoke.

'Lily, I been caught,' she said with a little sob.

I frowned. 'What do you mean, caught? Caught what?'

She sighed heavily, a little sob escaping her lips. 'I'm up the duff. 'Aving a baby. Oh, Lily, what am I going to do?'

Hardly able to breathe, I stood still for a minute, trying to take in what she'd said. I spotted a pub nearby and pulled her into it. It was early so the place was nearly empty and even the landlord wasn't about, although we heard him clattering about somewhere. The lino was sticky and our feet made sucking noises as we walked. Small circular tables were decorated with stained beer mats, but the fire on one wall was burning cheerfully. I took Mavis to a table near it so we could keep warm.

She avoided my eye, and I saw her gulp back tears.

'Oh, Mavis, that's such bad luck. What do you think you'll do?' I put my hand on hers.

She blinked rapidly trying to hold back tears. 'Dunno, I can't go 'aving a nipper, not now, I ain't got no bloke nor nothing.'

'Won't the bloke stand by you?' I asked.

Her eyes filled with tears. 'I don't know who it was. Remember that night at the dance when I went outside for a while? It was then.'

I did remember, that was the time she talked about going up against a wall. 'Didn't you use a johnny?'

She gave a bitter laugh. 'Yeah, I made sure 'e did, but the bloody thing only split, didn't it. But just the once, we only did it the once and I ain't been with no one else. Got to be 'im and I have no idea who 'e is.'

Just then the landlord appeared, his hands full of beer glasses. 'Sorry, ladies, I didn't hear you come in. What can I get you?' He put the glasses down and started to hang them up while we made up our mind. 'Two halves of shandy please,' I said, going over to get them.

Mavis drank hers down in one go. 'I've got to get rid of it,' she said, her eyes sliding away from mine. She held up her glass. 'Can I have a gin please?'

I was taken aback. 'A gin? Since when did you drink gin?'

She bit her lip. 'Drinking gin in a 'ot bath is supposed to do the trick, but I've done it twice and nothing happened. Three weeks late now and my boobies are getting bigger and sore. Perhaps another gin'll take my mind off it if nothing else.'

I went over to get her drink wondering how on earth she would cope with a baby. She was the same age as me and I couldn't imagine having that responsibility.

The landlord got the gin. 'One for you as well?' he asked, wiping the bar. 'You should keep your friend company.'

An elderly couple came in. He walked slowly with a stick and she was so bent over I wondered how she saw where she was going. They smiled hello to the landlord. 'Hello, James, hello, Mary. The usual?' he said, getting their drinks without needing to ask what they wanted.

I walked over to sit next to Mavis again. 'Mavis, what are you going to do?'

She started to count things off on her fingers. 'Well, done the gin and 'ot baths; jumped up and down a million times; washed high walls; drunk a whole bottle of cod liver oil and didn't get off the toilet for a day; eaten food so spicy it made my eyes water. Nothing worked. I've got to do something more drastic.'

'Won't your family help you with a baby?' I asked.

She shrugged. 'Probably, but there'd be a price to pay. I'd never 'ear the end of it. Bringing shame to their name – like we've got a good one anyway – costing hard-earned dosh with another mouth to feed. It'll go on and on for ever. They'd never let me forget it. No, I've got to get rid of it. I don't want a baby anyway.'

I checked we couldn't be overheard. 'Keep your voice down, Mavis. It's dangerous to do anything illegal like that. You might die or go to prison.'

Her chin jutted out. 'I'd rather die. It'd be the end of all my dreams. I want to come to Paris with you lot. I may not be clever but I want to see new places and try new things. I don't want a nipper dragging me down, ruining everything.'

We talked and talked about it, but there was no changing her mind.

With a heavy heart, I thought of my nurse friend Jean and what she'd told me. 'A friend of mine might know about someone you can go to. But she says it's really dangerous.'

The chin jutted again. 'I don't care. Can you get me the address?'

* * *

After a big lecture about the dangers and the fact that abortions were illegal, Jean gave me a couple of addresses for Mavis. It took a lot of persuasion, but when I told her how desperate Mavis was she relented. She'd heard of too many girls in Mavis's condition who'd killed themselves. Patients she'd cared for after their abortions went wrong had given her the names of the abortionists, even though she didn't want to know. One was a doctor, but he was so expensive that even if I gave Mavis all my savings and she put what little she had in too, there was no way she could afford him. The other was an old midwife living in a run-down part of town.

'She's probably better than the doctor,' Jean said, 'I've seen what the doctor does to girls and it's like he's punishing them. Most of them will never be able to have children after he's finished with them.'

5

MAVIS

Two days later, Mavis and I found the address Jean had given us. We stood outside looking at the broken windows and rubbish strewn around the tenement building. Weeds grew out of the roof and some tiles were hanging loose. Dirty kids were kicking a ball around on the street outside. Two had no shoes and one wore only a grubby jumper and had no knickers, despite the cold.

I held Mavis's hand, which trembled slightly.

'Are you sure you want to do this? I'm really scared for you. Please think again. What about having the baby adopted?'

'I'd still 'ave to have it first, wouldn't I? Have to live with my mum when I was too big to work. Ruin all my plans. I know you're being kind Lily, but I gotta do this.' She pulled my hand, dragging me towards the front door. It had been painted green many years ago, but it was hard to tell now. The paint was flaking off. Kids had drawn rude things on it and people had written messages and stuck posters advertising things for sale, or the services of ladies of the night. It groaned as we opened it and the noise reminded me of the horror films we used to see at the Dream Palace. I held my breath, half-expecting to see an alien or a man with arm raised up ready to strike. But all there was was a dirty hallway. Under the stairs there was a pram, a bike with a wheel missing and a pile of old newspapers.

I got out the slip of paper I'd written the address on. 'It's number thirty-seven,' I whispered.

We started up the stairs. They were sticky and smelled strongly of wee. I put my hand on the banister and then removed it again quickly, getting my hankie out and wiping my hand clean as best I could.

Thirty-seven was on the third floor and we heard a radio playing and saw a light under the door.

'Sure?' I asked for the umpteenth time.

By way of answer, Mavis took a deep breath and knocked three times. The door was promptly opened by a plump lady wearing a flowery apron, her hair tied up with a scarf knotted at the front. She dragged us in quickly and locked the door behind us.

'Which of you is it?' she asked.

'Me.' Mavis said in a voice so weak it was hard to hear.

'And you are?' she said, turning to me. 'I'm Lily, Mavis's friend.'

'Well, sit yourself down, girls. I'll make us a tea and you can drink it while I get the stuff ready. You do understand you can never, ever tell anyone about this, don't you? We'll all end up in prison, and then I'll never be able to help any other girls in your situation, Mavis. Are we all agreed on that?'

The room was in better condition that I'd have expected, seeing as how bad the rest of the building was. The walls had flowery wallpaper and there were red and blue rag rugs on the wooden floor. Her bed was in one corner with a well-washed blue candlewick bedspread reaching down to the floor. A tiny area on the wall opposite served as a kitchen. She had a sink with a cold tap, a gas ring and a table covered with a blue oilcloth. People in the next flat started to argue about money. There was a loud bang, the arguing stopped, then started again.

As the midwife warmed the pot, she looked over her shoulder. 'You can call me Mrs Smith, not my real name, but it'll do. If you need the lavvy, it's up one floor on the left.'

'I'm going to go,' Mavis said, standing up, 'nerves getting the better of me.'

When she got back, Mrs Smith handed her the tea. 'First things first. You got the money?'

Mavis reached into her pocket and pulled out an envelope. 'It's all there.'

Mrs Smith counted the notes, nodded and then put the money and envelope in a drawer in the table.

Business done, she became softer. 'I know this is hard for you,' she said looking at Mavis, 'but it'll soon be done and you can get on with your life.'

Mavis wiped her eyes and nodded silently. She was so white it was as if someone had sucked all the energy out of her.

'Now let me tell you what's going to happen. You can see over there—' she nodded to the gas ring '—I've got my equipment boiling for a few minutes to make sure it's clean. You don't need to know what it is, you won't even see it. And you—' she nodded to me '—you can hold Mavis's hand, but I suggest you look the other way. I don't want anyone fainting on me.'

I felt cold and clammy at the thought of what was going to happen. Suppose Mavis died? What if she wished afterwards that she'd kept the baby? Suppose the police found out somehow and we all ended up in prison? My mind wouldn't keep quiet, it kept going over and over all the awful things that might happen. 'Do I have to see it?' Mavis asked Mrs Smith.

She shrugged. 'How many weeks are you?'

Mavis put her hand to her stomach, 'I'm a month late,' she said.

'Only a month? Nothing to see yet, too small. You don't have anything to worry about.' She went over to the gas ring and poured the boiling water into a washing-up bowl. She used some wooden washing tongs to pick up her instruments. I looked away quickly; the less I saw, the less I'd have to remember. I turned to Mavis. 'Tell me something, anything, let's chat.'

But before we could do that Mrs Smith was putting an old blanket, an oilcloth and layers of newspapers on her bed.

'Right, this is what happens,' she said, 'you'll feel a sharp pain, but it only lasts a minute, then you'll start to bleed, but it won't be too bad. You might feel a bit rough for a day or two, but not everyone does. Finished your tea?'

Mavis stood up, her knees shaking and her lip quivering. She walked the few steps towards the bed as if being held back by a strong piece of elastic.

'Are you sure?' I asked, walking beside her, holding her hand. She didn't answer, but got on the bed as if it were her coffin.

'Take your knickers off and hitch up your skirt, dear,' Mrs Smith said, pushing back her sleeves. 'You got a hankie?'

Mavis nodded and got it out of her sleeve.

'Right, when I tell you, fold it up into a roll then put it in between your teeth. I can't have you making noise or the cops'll be all over us like a rash.'

I sat by Mavis's head, held her hand again and looked anywhere but where Mrs Smith was doing her grizzly work.

'Open your legs, dear. Wider, that's it. I can see nicely. Now hold your friend's hand tight, this won't take a minute. Hankie time.'

Mavis put the hankie in her mouth and seconds later she let out a muffled, anguished cry, her eyes big as half-crowns. Then there was silence. But she was breathing fast and when I squeezed her hand, she squeezed back.

Mrs Smith stood up and handed her an old well-washed tea towel. 'All done, dear. Now here's a cloth to put between your legs. Get your knickers back on.'

It was all over so quickly. One second Mavis was in the family way, and the next that was all over. I hoped against hope that she would never regret what happened.

She pulled her knickers back on over the cloth and blood trickled down her leg. She wiped it with her hankie and sat up, too wobbly to stand.

'Here, have a drink of water,' Mrs Smith said, handing her one, 'then you've got to leave. Can't have you here any longer than necessary. And remember, you never saw me, I never saw you. You must never come back here under any circumstances. Understand?'

'And we won't tell anyone,' I said quietly, 'not even our friends.'

Mavis shook her head, face still screwed tight in pain.

'Come on, dear. Out with you.' Mrs Smith said.

She helped her to her feet and gave her her coat.

We walked slowly back down the stairs, Mavis leaning heavily on my arm. The bus stop seemed much further than when we arrived and she got slower with every step. The bus stop was one of the news ones, art deco they called them. Rounded one end and lots of windows. But the most important thing was that it had a bench that Mavis could sit on.

On the bus five minutes later, a lady leaned over and tapped Mavis on the shoulder. 'You're bleeding, love,' she whispered, cupping her hand and speaking into Mavis's ear.

A blush rose on Mavis's face as she bent forward to wipe the blood, but worse was to come. When she stood up, she gasped, 'I'm bleeding, I'm really bleeding,' she said. There was a lot more than a trickle and the flow was getting faster. Spots of blood glistened on the floor – shiny, dangerous.

My mind was a whirl, Mrs Smith hadn't said anything about this. She said there'd be just a bit of blood but this was a lot more than a bit.

'What're we going to do?' Mavis whispered. 'She said we can't go back there.'

We got off the bus and sat on a wall, trying to stay out of the way of prying eyes. Mavis clutched my arm. 'Oh Lily, what can I do? If I go to hospital, they'll tell the police.' Even as she spoke her voice seemed to be getting weaker.

There was only one person I could trust. My friend Jean, the nurse. I stopped a cab and bundled Mavis in, hoping she wouldn't leave a trail of blood. 'St Mary's Hospital, please,' I said, thinking the fare would cost me all my spending money for the rest of the week.

When we arrived, I sat Mavis on a wall at the front of the building. 'I'm going to find my friend Jean if she's on duty and see if she will help. Will you be okay to wait here?'

She gave a weak smile. 'I'll just move along so I can rest me 'ead against this wall. I'll be 'ere when you get back. Don't be long.'

It took me ten minutes to find Jean's ward, then another ten minutes for her to get away from her duties.

I took her to one side and spoke quietly. 'I'm so grateful Jean. The woman said…'

'Don't tell me a thing,' she said, 'the less I know the better. We can take her in, it's up to the doctor whether he reports her to the police or not. A lot of them just pretend they think it's a miscarriage.'

We hurried back through the long corridors, dodging people walking slowly; wheelchairs; and porters pushing trolleys.

'There she is,' I said, pointing to Mavis who was leaning with her back against the wall.

She was unconscious, sitting in a pool of blood.

Jean felt her pulse. 'She's alive, but her pulse is very weak and irregular. Lay her down on the wall. I'll get a porter with a trolley.'

I was terrified Mavis would die before she got back.

Two hours later, after an emergency operation, Mavis was on the ward with a blood transfusion drip in her arm. Although it was past visiting time they let me sit with her for a while. She hadn't come round from the anaesthetic and even though the doctor said she would be okay, I was having trouble keeping back tears. I held her hand and thought how close she'd come to dying. She was such a brave, lively girl who had a tough start in life and deserved every chance to fulfil her dreams.

I looked at the ward clock. It was nine o'clock. The ward sister came over to me. 'Go on home now, she'll be fine. You can phone first thing in the morning to check up on her.'

I visited the next evening after training had finished, and was relieved to find Mavis much stronger. 'They let me use the phone and I phoned my mum. Didn't tell her what happened – just that I'd been poorly and wanted to come 'ome for a couple of days. She was all right with it as long as I remembered to take my ration card. The doctor says I'll be fine by the end of the week.'

I held her hand. 'Thank goodness for that. I was really worried we were going to lose you there for a little while.'

6

NEW POSTINGS

We were coming to the end of our training, when Miss Rounds called us together.

'Girls,' she said, 'I have just put your next postings on the wall next door. You may go to see them now if you so wish.'

Every single one of us hurried to the door, then, just like at basic training, pushed each other out of the way trying to see what fate awaited us.

I scanned the list, reading and rereading it to make sure I hadn't made a mistake. Then I turned to Amanda and Bronwyn, hardly able to speak. 'Yes! We're all going to Paris!'

'All right for some,' someone near me said, 'I'm going to Doncaster.'

I gave her a sympathetic look. 'I didn't think I'd get in,' I said, 'my French is still nowhere near as good as Amanda and Bronwyn's.'

Miss Rounds' voice made me jump. 'No, your French still leaves a lot to be desired, Volunteer Baker, and I have to tell you, you only got this posting because two of the girls there are ill and have had to be repatriated. You're the next best thing.'

I didn't mind at all being called the next best thing. We were going to Paris!

* * *

We stood gazing out at Dover from the side of the ship, jostling for space with all the soldiers going to France. The port was busy with sailors hurried here and there, kitbags on their shoulders; porters trundled boxes on to ships and women waved goodbye to their loved ones. The smell of the sea mixed with the smell of oil and greasy food. Voices shouted, whistled, sang. Heavy clouds loomed low, turning the scene a dull grey, then weighty raindrops began to fall.

Standing under cover out of the rain, Amanda, Bronwyn, Mavis and me waved as the boat started to slowly leave the dock. 'I don't know what we're waving for,' said Amanda, 'after all, we don't know anyone.'

'Doesn't matter, it's just something you have to do,' I said, grinning as the engines hummed. 'I'm so glad you got to come with us Mavis,' I said, squashed next to her.

'Bit last minute, wasn't it? An orderly again, but never mind, at least I'll be in Paris with you lot.'

'Do you know who you'll be an orderly for?' I asked.

'I think it's you lot and the army and BEF soldiers in the building. At least I'll get to know everyone.'

'You okay now?' I asked. She knew what I meant. 'Yeah, nothing to it. I'm fine.' I could see her holding back a tear.

'It's going to be a rough trip,' I heard someone near me say. My heart sank. I'd never been at sea before; the most I'd experienced was a pleasure trip on a river and I felt sure that wouldn't prepare me for this.

'Do you get seasick?' I asked the others.

Amanda thought for a minute. 'I've been across to France twice before, but the sea was always calm. I did feel a bit queasy once or twice though. What about you, Bronwyn?'

'It's like this see, my dad was a sailor, so surely I won't be seasick. Mind you, I've heard some sailors are sick for the whole journey.'

I patted the sturdy rail. 'This ship reminds me of the ones that lads sail on the pond near our house.' It was pointed at both ends with one funnel and two masts.

Mavis nodded. 'Someone told me this used to be a post office ship, but now it's military so they painted it grey.'

The rain got heavier, and squally winds blew the water into our shelter, driving us inside.

Within minutes the sea swell got worse and we had to sit to avoid falling over. Angry waves threw themselves at the side of the boat – water beating against the windows as if it was trying to break the glass and get in. The ship groaned and creaked like it was ready to fall apart any minute. The sky darkened; the gloom torn apart by flashes of lightning every few minutes. Sailors struggled to move around the deck, clutching onto anything lashed down. The deck awash with foam like popcorn that had escaped from its bag.

A sailor came round and handed out paper bags to be sick into. Soon the room filled with the sound of heaving and the throat-clenching smell of vomit. Bronwyn was right; she wasn't seasick, but Amanda, Mavis and I certainly were. We were torn between straining our muscles clutching onto our seats to avoid being thrown onto the metal floor, and holding the bags to our mouths.

'Do you think we'll sink?' I gasped between bouts of sickness.

Bronwyn grinned. 'Well, the sailors are okay, like. They're not worried so I suppose we shouldn't be either.'

For an hour we were at the mercy of the sea, thrown from side to side, barely able to hear each other for loud claps of thunder and the screeching of the boat. It was like the gods had decided to throw everything they had at us.

Then, as suddenly as it began, the storm lessened. Waves still battered the ship but they were getting less furious. The squealing of metal gradually calmed until we were able to tentatively stand upright again.

I put the sick bag in a bin and wiped my lips with my hankie, longing for some water to get rid of the taste in my mouth. 'Phew, I think we made it,' I said.

'Let's pray a Y-boat doesn't get us,' Amanda said, holding her hands in a prayer gesture.

She was right. I sent up a silent prayer to a God I wasn't sure I believed in.

7

PARIS

Driving into Paris was so exciting that the four of us didn't know where to look first, although Amanda had seen most of it before. I think the driver took pity on us and drove past as many sights as possible on the way to our billet.

'Look! The Eiffel Tower!' Bronwyn shouted, pointing. It was so impressive, towering elegantly over the city, but it was largely ignored by the people who just went about their everyday lives. When I thought about it, the same thing happened to Big Ben and the Houses of Parliament. A few tourists would always be there gaping, but the people who saw it every day didn't take any notice.

I was as interested in the people as I was in the sights. The women were all incredibly elegant with their high heels, slim skirts and clutch bags. Men and women strode purposefully down the boulevards as if going somewhere very important. I saw a group of men in turbans walking by and bicycles weaving in and out of the cars and lorries. Trolley buses stopped the traffic while they took on their customers, and we passed a flower market whose colourful blooms brightened the dull, overcast day. It was all so, well, French. I couldn't stop smiling.

'You'll love it here,' Amanda said. 'I know my way around and I can take us to the best places.'

Bronwyn laughed. 'Come on, Amanda, we're not your rich family. You'll have to take us to the best cheap places. Wonder how much free time we'll have, anyway.'

We stopped outside a tall, handsome building. It was painted a creamy colour and had double wooden doors that arched at the top with elaborate carving. Either side of the door were long windows. The building was five floors high.

It was to be our new home.

We rang a bell and the door was opened by a tiny woman who looked like a puff of wind would blow her over. Her hair was cut in a stylish bob and she wore a crisp white blouse and tailored trousers. I instantly wanted to be like her.

'*Bonjour, mes amis, mes soldierettes,*' she said, 'welcome. I am Clara and I am your French Liaison contact. I serve with the Fighting French Forces. Your apartment is on the third floor, I'm afraid. Many stairs to climb.'

We stepped inside the door and gaped. The entrance hall was massive with a marble floor and sparkling chandelier. An outsize brocade-covered chair with gold legs stood in one corner.

'*Venez,*' she said, 'follow me.'

We lugged our kitbags up the stairs, wondering who lived behind each door we passed. When we got to the third floor Clara opened the door with a flourish. We walked straight into the living room and stood looking around with our mouths open. The apartment was beautiful. High ceilings with elaborate coving gave the room a light, airy feel as did the huge windows overlooking the busy street. Brocade curtains pulled back with outsize tassels framed the windows, although I noticed blackout blinds rolled up at the top of each one. I don't know what the style of furniture was called, but it seemed very fancy and much too expensive to actually use.

'Make yourself comfortable,' Clara said. 'This will be your home for your time in Paris. You will share your rooms with two other girls. The other telephonists are in the apartment opposite.'

Bronwyn let out a low whistle. 'I'm going to say something serious now. They'd never believe this place back at home. They'd be green with envy.'

We walked to the window and stared at the scene below. An elderly, Jewish man with a long white beard, a wide brimmed black hat and a walking stick lay with his legs on a windowsill sleeping. Nearby, a young woman stood with a child on one hip and bunches of flowers for sale in the other hand. A chic woman stopped and bought a bunch, kissing the child who wiped the cheek she had kissed with his grubby sleeve. The noise of the traffic competed with the calls of newspaper sellers. Everything was so normal, you could forget war raged not very far away.

We had two bedrooms at the back of the flat, where windows overlooked a central courtyard with buildings all round. A gap between the buildings opposite was the way out to the street behind. Each bedroom had three beds. In each room one bed already had an owner. The bed had been slept in and clothes were piled neatly on the chair at the side of the bed that acted as a bedside table.

'Cor, only three of us, luxury after the bunkhouse,' Mavis said.

There was a bathroom with a huge bath on legs shaped like lion's feet. Black and white tiles covered the floor and the walls were pure white. It was heaven. I stood in the middle of the room the first time I used it, held my arms out, and spun round like a child, laughing. I thought our corporation house was fantastic after what we'd had before, but it was nothing compared to this. I thanked the day I met Bronwyn and her willingness to teach me French.

'Where are we in Paris?' I asked Clara. 'Are we near the centre?'

She smiled. '*Oui*, we are in the Marais. It is a very mixed area and also the area where many Jews live. Some have already left because of the Nazis, but many remain.'

Mention of the Nazis made us all take notice. 'Do you think the Germans will invade Paris?' Amanda asked.

Clara shrugged. '*Pas du tout.* In the last war they did not and we do not expect them to do so now. The government is not worried for Paris.'

'But I heard they are evacuating lots of children just like in London, and you've got gas masks too,' Bronwyn said.

'It is just a precaution, nothing to worry about. If the Germans do come towards our city, we will have plenty of time to leave. Put it out of your minds and enjoy your time here. Now, put your bags in the bedrooms and come upstairs to where you will work.'

The telephone room was a carbon copy of our flat, but without the comfortable furniture. The main room housed eight telephone switchboards and four were currently in use, their ATS operators sitting with their headsets in place, speaking quietly into them. As we walked in they waved a greeting and carried on.

A tall, mannish woman came from another room. She was wearing the uniform of an ATS Senior Commandant, and had steely hair pulled into a bun low on the back of her head.

'I'll take over now, Clara,' she said, 'thank you.'

As she turned to us, we stood to attention and saluted. 'At ease, girls,' she said, 'I'm Senior Commandant Perkins, but you can call me Mrs Perkins. As you know, you are attached to the British army and will be working for them and the British Expeditionary Force who have offices on the fourth floor. You'll meet them tomorrow.

You must be tired after your journey, but I knew you'd want to see where you will be working. We work in shifts so that we can answer the phones twenty-four hours a day. We'll break you in gently, and tomorrow you can each shadow the girls on duty so you get to know the ropes and who's who. I would introduce you to the girls here, but they're all busy. You'll have plenty of time to get to know each other. Now, do you have any questions?'

I put my hand up. 'Mrs Perkins, are we allowed out of the building?'

She blinked in surprise. 'Of course, my dear, this isn't a prison. But you must take the greatest care never to talk about anything you learn here. It is believed there are German spies everywhere. Careless talk costs lives. Now, I'm not the sort of senior leader who shouts and humiliates my girls, but I still expect total profession-alism at all times, or there will be repercussions. Do we under-stand each other?'

We all nodded, and I wondered what the repercussions might be. We wouldn't be court-martialled, but we might be sent back to Blighty. Even after a few hours in Paris, I wanted to make sure that didn't happen. I was longing to get to know the city better and improve my French. I wondered if Edward was in Paris. The odds on us being in the same place at the same time were too big to think about, but I fully intended to keep searching for him amongst the soldiers we came across. I was horrified to realise it was becoming harder to remember his face.

A door opened and a man in officer's uniform came in. He was tiny; only about five foot four and as thin as he was short. He had green eyes and mousy-brown hair cut very short.

He nodded to Mrs Perkins. 'Now, girls,' she said, 'this is Lieu-tenant Smith. Amongst other things, he is in charge of security. He wants to take this opportunity to say a few words.'

She stood aside and let him take charge. He ushered us to the other side of the room away from where the telephonists were working.

'Good evening, ladies. Mrs Perkins will have given you some information about our work, but much of it must remain secret to you even though you put calls through. The work we do upstairs is extremely important to the war effort. If you accidentally overhear something, it must never be repeated, even to each other. Do you understand?'

He had a bit of food between his front teeth and dandruff on his collar so it was difficult to listen to him without wanting to laugh, but we nodded dutifully.

'This means as soon as you transfer a call, you disconnect. No listening in under any circumstances.'

I was beginning to feel irritated. What he was saying was so obvious it was almost insulting. In any case, we had had a lecture about all this during our training.

'If you write anything down, for example a name or a telephone number, you must give it to Mrs Perkins at the end of your shift and she will ensure it is properly destroyed. We have local cleaners and although they are vetted, we can never take anything for granted, so everything must be properly dealt with. I will be coming down regularly to check on security. Any questions?'

We all shook our heads. I was pretty sure the others were like me, fed up with this pompous little man and ready for our beds. It had been a long day.

Bronwyn and I shared one bedroom along with whoever was in the third bed. Mavis and Amanda shared another with someone else they hadn't met yet. Later that evening Bronwyn and I met our room-mate, an ATS girl called Ingrid. I wondered if she had been in Paris long because she had the air of a Parisian. She was tall and slim with perfect hair and even in her uniform she would stand out in a crowd.

'Lovely to meet you both,' she said, 'always good to meet new people. We're a friendly bunch and we even mix with the officers upstairs sometimes. We'll see a lot of each other because Mrs Perkins tries to put room-mates on the same shift if she can. Unless we hate each other, of course!'

'I'm sure we won't,' I said, smiling. 'Have you been in Paris long?'

She sat on her bed and unlaced her shoes. 'Only three weeks but I'm finding my way round. I'll show you if you like.'

I soon found out that we rarely got a whole day off, but with our shifts we were sometimes free in the evening and sometimes during the day. I soon grew to hate the night shift, finding it hard to stay awake. I was to learn more about Ingrid that first night. She snored like a trooper. I resolved to find some earplugs as quickly as possible.

Our alarm went off at 6 a.m. What with basic training and factory work, I was used to getting up early. Amanda was on a different shift but had to get up to be shown the ropes with us. Mavis had quite different duties, so her shifts didn't overlap neatly with ours.

'Did I really hear snoring through your wall?' Amanda asked.

I groaned, 'Got any earplugs?'

* * *

The first time we had an afternoon free, Bronwyn and I decided to explore the city. We didn't go with Ingrid because she had already gone out. 'There's a pity,' Bronwyn said, 'she'd have been helpful, but at least we've got a map.'

I nodded. 'And the underground can't be too difficult to find our way round. Where shall we go first?'

'The Champs-Élysées,' she said without a second's hesitation, 'let's window shop.'

We walked past glittering shops full of unaffordable clothes made by famous designers. On the pavement, street-sellers plied their goods.

'Hey,' I said to Bronwyn, feeling shocked, 'that couple are selling packets of dirty postcards.'

She chuckled. 'Ingrid told me about them. They say they're dirty postcards so the lechy old men buy them, but they're not. They're ordinary postcards of Paris under the top one.'

I frowned. 'But wouldn't they complain?'

'What? Come back and show themselves up complaining about buying dirty postcards? What do you think?'

Yet again, I realised what a sheltered life I'd led.

But window-shopping gets boring after a while when you've no money to buy anything, so we decided we'd just wander round backstreets. If we got lost, it would be an adventure.

As we stepped into the first narrow lane, a skinny black cat stood guard as if it wasn't going to let us through. I bent down to stroke it but it hissed, back arched, and ran into an alleyway. We peered after it.

'Blimey, just streets away from the expensive shops and what a difference,' Bronwyn said.

The alleyway was a chasm of tall, dirty buildings leaning towards each other at crazy angles like rotting teeth in a drunk's mouth. Grey washing hung limply from windows, and dirty kids kicked around an old ball, their shouts echoing against the high walls. An old lady sat in a doorway. She wore a flowery pinny topped with an old grey blanket, and her thin, grey hair was tied up in a cotton scarf knotted at the top. She was peeling potatoes, the tin bowl held between her knees. Smells of garlic, onions and sewage drifted along the alleyway.

We heard an argument from one of the higher floors, then the sound of a slap followed by another louder, slap.

A head appeared from a window opposite. 'For Christ's sake, shut up you two!' a woman shouted, waving her fist.

'They're not all rich in Paris, then,' I said quietly.

'Nah, they've had a recession too, just like us, poor sods,' Bronwyn said.

We continued walking past blocks of flats. Some were fairly modern, but it was clear the people who lived in them were poor. We passed a once dignified square and in the corner saw a queue of people waiting by one of the buildings.

'That must be where they can get soup for free,' Bronwyn said.

We walked past the queue of hungry people, feeling bad that we were well fed and clothed. 'Let's do something to help the poor on our time off,' I said.

She stopped in her tracks. 'You're joking, aren't you? My fami-ly'd be the ones queueing for handouts.'

'Then you know how much that help means. We might come from poor families, but now we're lucky. We've got regular jobs, uniform provided and enough food. I'm going to try to find something I can do to help for three or four hours a week.'

'But what about our shifts?' she asked. 'You'll never be able to do anything regular.'

I sighed. 'I don't know, but I can ask Clara. We won't have enough money to be going out all the time and we can feel good doing something useful. We'll meet interesting people, that's for sure.'

Bronwyn grunted. 'Might get fleas, too,' she said. 'I'll think about it.'

By a strange coincidence we rounded the corner and came

across a flea market. There must have been a hundred people selling all sorts of things. Some just had one type of thing; clothes or books or something. They usually had a table to put their stuff on, and a chair to sit on. Others seemed like they were selling things they used every day: saucepans, blankets, shoes, pencils and crucifixes all thrown together on a sheet – their owners sitting on the ground desperate for a sale.

'Great!' said Bronwyn, heading for the nearest clothes stall. 'Let's buy some French clothes!'

We spent half an hour riffling through the clothes on a dozen stalls, but most were too badly made or too worn out to buy. 'Check the seams!' Bronwyn urged before we handed over our francs – after bartering, of course. I got a blouse that just needed a bit of mending, and Bronwyn got a brown jumper with a little flower embroidered on the sleeve. No fleas.

Sad that we didn't find any clothes to make us as elegant as Clara, we went to a little café where all types of workmen came in, many still carrying their tools and wearing their working clothes. One, a sturdy man not much taller than me, smelled as if he worked in a sewer. As he sat down, other people edged away from him. If he noticed, he was used to it. He drank a whole litre of wine in the time it took us to drink our tiny coffee, then walked out as if it had no impact on him.

'Hard to get a cup of tea in this country, isn't it?' I said.

'Getting hard to get a proper one at home too.' Bronwyn replied. 'This is the real Paris, not them fancy shops that most people can't afford to use anyway, I suppose.' She glanced out of the window and frowned. 'Hey, isn't that Ingrid?' She was right. Ingrid was close to an alleyway over the road. She checked left and right as if making sure she wasn't being followed, then darted in. She hadn't come out when we left fifteen minutes later.

* * *

'Hey, we saw you earlier,' I said to Ingrid when I was getting into bed. After the straw 'biscuit' mattress in the bunkhouse, having a proper mattress again made getting into bed feel a real luxury.

She spun on her heel. 'You saw me? Where?'

I was a bit taken aback by her sharp tone. 'Oh dear, I've no idea of the name of the road. Me and Bronwyn were in a little café near a flea market, about ten minutes' walk from here.'

Her shoulders relaxed and she smiled. 'That'll be when I went to drop off some papers for them upstairs,' she said, indicating the officers' office on the floor above us.

I wondered what papers would need to be taken to a down-at-heel alleyway, but it was none of my business and anyway, careless talk and all that. I didn't ask more questions.

The next day brought a lot of mail that must have been stacked up goodness knows where. Still no letter from Edward but there was one in writing I didn't recognise. I tore it open.

> Dear Lily,
>
> I thought I should let you know that Edward has been taken prisoner-of-war somewhere in Germany. Naturally the army notified me as next of kin. I have no further details.
>
> Yours,
>
> Mrs John Halpern

I fell back heavily on my bed. Edward a prisoner! I'd heard that they did terrible things to prisoners of war. My lovely Edward. I started to tremble violently. Bronwyn noticed and came over to me. 'What is it, *bach*? What's happened?'

My hand shaking, I passed the letter to her. She quickly read it.

'Now, take a deep breath,' she said, 'then another deep breath. Look into my eyes and breathe out slowly. Now drink this water.'

I had no idea if she knew what she was doing, but my shakes subsided and my brain cleared a bit. 'Will I be able to write to him, do you think?'

Bronwyn's bottom lip jutted. 'I'd keep writing if I was you, who knows if he'll get it? But it'd be bad if you haven't written. His mum's not a great writer, is she? Doesn't waste words.'

'She doesn't approve of me, that's why she's like that. I'm not high class enough for her son.'

Bronwyn stood up and pulled my hand. 'She'll learn to love you like we all do.'

'Do you think I should write back?'

Bronwyn thought for a minute. 'Yes, write back. If you always do the right thing, she can't complain about you.'

'But what if she doesn't write back?'

Bronwyn snorted. 'Then she's a very rude woman and you can feel superior to her. Just drop her a little note. Now come and have a cuppa. It'll take your mind off it for now and we can talk about it some more. Okay?'

Before I settled down to try to sleep I wrote a long letter to Edward.

My darling Edward,

Your mother has just let me know that you are in a prisoner-of-war camp and I am so worried about you. We hear such awful things that the Germans do and I hope that none of them are happening to you. I miss you so much; your gentle hug, your kind voice and your lovely sense of humour. I always kiss my ring before I go to sleep. It's the most wonderful thing I've ever owned because you gave it to me.

I hope you have got my earlier letters telling you that I'm a telephonist now. I wondered what had happened because I hadn't heard from you for some time. At least you're alive and that is the best news I could possibly ever have. I can't say where I am, of course, but I am lucky enough to be here with the three girls I told you about – Bronwyn, Amanda and Mavis. We're also getting to know the other telephonists who work here. We have to concentrate all the time, but we are aware that it is much easier work than many people have during this wretched war.

I often think about our time together. Do you remember how we met, when you got my handbag back from that thief ? I thought you were a hero then, and I still think that. I thank my lucky stars that I met you.

I will write regularly even though I have no idea if you will receive these letters.

Take care my darling, I love you, Lily xxx

I kissed the letter and put it in an envelope ready for posting. As I tried to sleep images kept flashing into my mind of Edward starving, or being tortured or worse. I woke up to find my pillow wet.

'I heard you getting upset last night,' Ingrid said next day as we were getting ready for our shift. 'Bad news?'

I gulped back a tear. 'My fiancé has been taken prisoner of war.'

'That's tough,' she said, picking up her bag, 'come on, or we'll be late.'

* * *

Every Friday evening, those of us who weren't on duty were invited to join the soldiers working in the building, for sherry. We met in their office on the floor above us. The layout was familiar to us now, but I noticed that they had a nice rug under each desk and that their desks were better quality than ours – officers' desks. It was very unsettling mixing with the officers; up until then they'd just been people who gave me orders. Strange that it should feel awkward because Edward is an officer; but then he was my Edward.

The drinks evening started very formally with small glasses of sherry and slices of French bread with cheese. The girls who had been there longer were more at ease and so was Amanda – I guess she was used to speaking to high-ups. I was better than I used to be, but still needed more confidence to speak to some people. I stood around and waited to be spoken to rather than start conversations myself. Talk was mostly of the war and the advances the Germans were making. It was depressing. After a couple of sherries we all got more relaxed and ended up going to Henri's Bar across the street. Thank goodness the conversation got more informal and people spoke about their families and their hopes for the future.

Henri's was a gloomy place, thick with the smoke of Gitanes – the ceiling sticky brown. Posters urged us to drink Amer Picon Aperitif, while others reminded us to wear our gas masks. The skinny, oily-haired barman had great expertise at talking with a ciggie in his mouth – absent-mindedly brushing away the ash that fell onto his jumper from time to time. It was peppered with tiny burns like it had measles or flea bites. It made me grimace, remembering the flea incident in the hotel in London.

I sat next to George, a lower-level officer, who was very keen to buy me and Bronwyn drinks.

'Are you enjoying your new posting?' he asked.

He reminded me of Edward. The same kind smile and sparkling blue eyes. He was also very friendly and a good listener.

'Did you notice George was giving you a lot of attention?' Bronwyn asked with a wink, when we got back to our room.

'No, he didn't, he was talking to both of us,' I said.

She chuckled. 'I'm going to tell you the truth now. I might as well not have been there. You've got yourself an admirer.'

My initial reaction was a warm glow. George found me attractive. After all these weeks in uniform, I hardly thought of myself as a woman at all, never mind one who a man might want to spend time with. I started to smile, then brought myself up short. Edward; I'd never be unfaithful to Edward, not even in my head.

'I'd better avoid him then, I'm engaged after all.'

Bronwyn just raised one eyebrow by way of reply. 'Hey,' she said, 'did you see how Ingrid was sucking up to that old bloke?'

'Commander Thomas?'

'Not being funny or nothing, but I think she fancies him and if the bulge in his trousers was anything to go by, he felt the same.'

'Bronwyn!' I said, my voice squeaking. 'Fancy noticing that. You are a one.'

She grinned. 'Hard to miss it, sweetheart, you were too busy talking to your new admirer.'

A picture of Commander Thomas came into my mind. He was at least sixty with a stomach that almost reached his knees and eyebrows like a wicker basket.

'She can't possibly fancy him,' I said. 'Is he rich or something?'

She picked up her soap bag and dressing gown. 'No accounting for taste, *cariad*, perhaps he reminds her of her dad. Or granddad.'

* * *

Marie-Claude was everyone's idea of a jolly French cook. Her plump backside wobbled like a pair of heavy balloons as she walked and her generous stomach was covered by a fresh flowery apron each day. She was in charge of the soup kitchen where I volunteered occasionally, preparing one hot meal a day for the many starving people in Paris. Her ready smile and her ability to remember the names of most of the people she served brightened their day and was a good role model for us helpers.

Not that it was all sweetness and light.

'Can't you peel quicker!' she said, wiping her face with a damp tea towel. 'We need to get those potatoes on now or they'll be queueing and giving us hell.'

I wondered if I'd ever work quickly enough for Marie-Claude. But she had to get me and two other volunteers, Paul and Evette, working at top speed to get the meals ready on time. Our 'guests' were people of all nationalities, who were often gaunt and weak from lack of food. Paul told me he volunteered because he only had ten francs to his name and it meant he got one meal a day. He was thin enough for that to be true. Several inches taller than me, I would have bet that he didn't weigh any more – his skin was pasty and dull and his hair hung lank around his neck.

One day he realised I'd seen him put a parcel in his coat. 'I won't eat until tomorrow without this,' he said. 'I can just about pay the rent on my room for another two weeks, then I'll be out on the streets.'

Evette walked up as we were speaking. 'Got anything to pawn?' she asked.

'Only my coat and I wear that at night to keep out the cold. The window in my room is broken and my landlady won't do a damn thing about it. And bugs! Don't talk to me about bugs! They eat me alive every night.'

Unconsciously, we all started to scratch.

'Put pepper round your bed,' Evette said, scratching her neck, 'They hate it so they'll leave you alone. Ask Marie-Claude if she can spare some.'

Paul buttoned up his coat, the bulge of the food parcel barely noticeable. 'Heard of any jobs?' he asked Evette.

She shook her head. 'You know I'd tell you if I heard anything.'

'Two months I've been searching. Two months! I've been after every job I've heard about and knocked on dozens of doors. Some of the bastards ask me for money before they'll even consider me for a job. Like I'd need a job if I had money!'

Evette touched his arm. 'It's not you – it's that there are so many other people fighting for every job.'

In the kitchen, the rubbish bin was always full by mid-morning and vegetable peel and other refuse accumulated on the floor round it like a rotting skirt. The only toilet was down a long, cobwebby corridor and it never flushed properly, so it always reeked. The place for hand washing was the sink that seemed to be perpetually full of washing-up. I soon learned that it was impossible to rely on having hot water, and sometimes we had to scrape the grease off plates with old bits of newspaper before washing them in cold water.

By the end of each shift I'd peeled a sack of potatoes and my hands were so wrinkled they were like bleached prunes. I helped to dish up the food too; a small plate of stew with a little unrecognisable meat for each person, along with a chunk of bread. I could have cried as I saw them queuing.

'You get used to it, *cherie*,' Paul said. 'It shows you have a good heart if you are upset, but you must learn to harden it just a little. Most of these people have nothing, just the clothes they stand up in. If they had anything else it will be at the pawnbrokers, like most of my stuff.'

'Do they ever get them back?' I asked.

He shook his head. 'If they manage to get a bit of work, they might get them back, but the next time they are out of work, they hock them again. It's the way of the world. *N'est-ce pas?*'

I knew about pawnbrokers, loads of people used them where we used to live, although my mum and dad had always scraped by without. But the parents of my friend Jean, the nurse, used them and sometimes small bits of furniture would vanish from her house for a while, then reappear later with not a thing said.

'Do you have a boyfriend back in England?' Paul asked.

I bit my lip. 'I'm engaged, but Edward, my fiancé, is a prisoner-of-war. I've been told he's in Germany but I don't know where and I haven't heard from him for ages.' I sniffed and wiped my eyes.

'That is very sad for you, *ma cherie*. I heard somewhere that in some camps the Nazis allow letters to prisoners who behave well. We can hope that he is one of them and you get a letter soon. It is very good of you to help in this kitchen.'

I was touched by his concern, 'I wish I could do it more often, but my shifts aren't always at the right time.'

I told Bronwyn and Amanda what he'd said next time we were together. We were walking along by the Seine on the Left Bank. Booksellers had wooden boxes on the stone wall for as far as I could see. It was a hot day for the time of year and wispy clouds seemed like they'd been drawn on the clear blue sky by a child with a horsehair broom that had lost most of its bristles. An elderly stall owner took off his hat, fanned his face, and wiped his forehead with his hankie. A customer two stalls down unpeeled his damp fingers from the book he was inspecting and got a dirty look for his trouble from the bookseller.

'Do you think he's right about Edward being allowed to write if he behaves?' I asked.

'I'm not sure what to think,' Amanda said. 'Of course, you want to get his letters but there's a bit of me that hopes the prisoners are not behaving well. Why make life easy for those damn Nazis?'

Bronwyn grunted. 'Are you crazy? The Nazis will have no hesitation in shooting anyone who...'

She stopped and a blush rose from her neck. 'Oh Lily, me and my big mouth. I'm so sorry, I'm sure he's alive and well. It's like this, I'm going to change the subject now. I heard there was another flea market round here. Let's go and see if we can find some nice clothes. We might have better luck this time.'

Just like the first flea market Bronwyn and I found before, there was the usual mixture of sellers – professionals, and people so down on their luck that even the pawnbrokers wouldn't lend on the sad rags of clothes they were trying to sell. In one corner there was a cluster of food stalls – the smell of cooking mingling with the smell of the old clothes, sweat and cigarettes.

I picked up a very old leather purse, much battered around the edges, and decided to buy it, just to give the elderly couple sitting on the floor some money without them losing their dignity.

I held it up to ask the price when the woman said, 'Is that you? The lady who gives out the food? It's me, Esme. We had little talk last time, *ja*? This is my husband, Fabio.'

It took me a few seconds to recognise her, not surprising when we saw each person only long enough to hand them a plate of food. Then I remembered she was crying as she queued and she told me she was worried about her family still in Germany.

'We left last year,' she had said, stifling a sob. 'After Kristall-nacht it was too dangerous to stay. But my brother and his family, they wouldn't leave and we don't know what's happened to them.'

I had squeezed her hand as I passed her the plate but there was no time to talk more because the people behind her in the queue were pushing and grumbling.

The folds of skin on her face and arms and her thin baggy dress showed she'd once been a much bigger woman. Fabio had the same haunted expression, although he managed a pale smile. 'He doesn't speak much French yet,' Esme said. 'I am glad to see you again. We have seen you in the street with a girl with a yellow jumper a few days ago. Is she one of your friends?'

I smiled. 'Yes, that is Ingrid, she works with me. I'm sorry if we didn't see you. I didn't mean to ignore you.'

She shook her head. 'No, no, you must not worry. We were across the road so you would not have seen us. Very strange, but later that day we saw the girl again. Ingrid, did you say? She had that jumper on again, it is very smart, I would love one like that. She was coming out of a little hotel with a much older man. Perhaps he was her father.'

Esme's husband tapped her on the arm, and said something to her. She listened then turned to me. 'He said, we cannot offer you food, but he would be very honoured if you would come to our room for a cup of tea one day.'

I felt humbled. These people had nothing, but they still wanted to share. 'I'd love to,' I said, 'let's arrange it next time I see you. But I'd better get back to my friends now.'

Groaning and holding her aching back, she stood up and came over, kissing me on both cheeks in true Parisian style. She smelled of sour milk and stale onions.

'*Shavua tov,*' she called after me as I left. I had no idea what it meant, but I waved and smiled as I searched for the others.

'Who were they?' Bronwyn asked when I caught up with her and Amanda.

'A couple who come to the meal kitchen. They're worried about their family in Germany.'

Amanda shook her head. 'They should be worried about themselves too. I know no one believes the Nazis will invade Paris but just because it didn't happen in the last war doesn't mean it won't in this one. Then they might well be in danger.'

I caught my breath. 'Do you think I should warn them? What if I'm worrying them for no good reason?'

Bronwyn interrupted. 'Let's find out as best we can how far into France the Nazis are...'

'Can't we just read the newspapers or listen to the radio?' I said.

'Well, I'm not being funny or anything,' she went on, getting a Gitane out of her pocket and lighting it, 'but I don't think you can trust what you hear like that. Governments don't always tell the truth, do they? Perhaps we could be a bit slow disconnecting when we put through calls occasionally. See what we can overhear.'

I was horrified. 'But that's spying!'

'Don't be silly, girl. We're not going running to the Germans to tell them are we? We wouldn't even tell that family you know. But we might find out when to warn them to leave without being too specific.'

I looked at Amanda. 'What do you think?'

She shrugged. 'It would only be a minute or two when we connect...'

'But they'd be able to hear the noise in our office.'

'Not if we put our hand over the mouthpiece,' Bronwyn said.

I was still doubtful. 'Well, only if it's just us on duty, otherwise the others might think we really are spies.'

Over the next week we overlapped on duty three times. Every time I listened to a bit of conversation I felt as if someone was nearby seeing everything I was doing. It was a waste of time anyway because I never heard anything interesting. Most people were still on the 'how are you' bit of the conversation when I pulled the plug. A lot of the time it wasn't possible to listen to more because other people were on duty with us.

Then, after the next duty day, Bronwyn caught up with me as we left the office. 'Come for a walk,' she said, speaking out of the side of her mouth like a criminal.

It was early afternoon so we had the luxury of the rest of the day to ourselves. 'Is Amanda coming?' I asked.

'No, she's busy writing letters home and Mavis is on a different shift, mostly working upstairs. It's just you and me, kid. Where shall we go?'

'Sacré Coeur,' I said immediately, 'we haven't been there yet.'

We got a bus, then walked quite a way to the cathedral. It was a cold day, but sunny and crisp. We stopped in the Square Marcel Bleustein Blanchet on our way and sat outside a little café warming our hands on steaming hot chocolate that smelled as good as it tasted. Despite the beautiful church there, it was a small oasis of calm in the busy city with few people wandering around. We heard traffic from nearby streets and a flock of birds flew over, probably returning from their winter homes, but otherwise it was just a gentle flow of people walking across the square from time to time.

Checking no one might overhear, I leaned towards Bronwyn. 'Come on then, what did you want to tell me?'

She looked around. 'Well, you know we was joking about Ingrid and that old geezer? Well, I heard someone asking him if he was still having a bit of you-know-what with the girl at work. Got to be her, hasn't it!'

I sat back in my chair, frowning. 'Commander Thomas? Blimey. But why would she? He's old enough to be her father.' Then I remembered what Esme said. 'Do you remember that couple I spoke to in the flea market? Esme said she'd seen Ingrid coming out of a hotel with a much older man. She thought he might be her father.'

Bronwyn shrugged. 'Yeah, and pigs might fly. Perhaps she's one of those girls who likes to collect scalps.'

'I wonder if he's a sugar daddy, buying her stuff.'

'She does have some nice jewellery and handbags.' Bronwyn clapped her hands and laughed.

'That'll be it. And I know he's married so she won't have to —

worry about him getting too attached. Use them and spit them out, like. Wouldn't mind a sugar daddy myself come to that, but he'd have to be a lot younger than hers. What do you think of her?'

I paused to think about that. 'Not sure, she's sometimes friendly and other times a bit remote.'

'She told you much about herself?' Bronwyn asked.

'Come to think of it, she hasn't. I'll have to ask her.'

Hot chocolate finished, we walked on towards Sacré Coeur. We wandered around Montmartre, weaving in and out of the little lanes. We tried to see inside Bricktop's Jazz Club but the door was firmly locked. In one lane we saw men in threadbare suits searching through rubbish bins for food, while others pocketed cigarette stubs from the ground. Yet within a couple of minutes we passed a café full of expensively dressed couples; women in fur wraps and men in homburgs being served dainty patisserie and coffee by perfectly uniformed waiters. The smells of the pastries and drinks mingled with the acrid smell of cigarette smoke. Across the road a street artist was painting the café scene watched by a couple of women in cloche hats and smart suits. One street seemed to house several artists' studios and we got a brief glimpse through the windows as we walked past.

'Well, I never,' Bronwyn said, stopping in her tracks at one studio, 'life classes. Did you see that? That woman had no clothes on. Bet she had goose pimples.'

I hadn't realised how much Sacré Coeur dominated the landscape with its position on a hill. We stood gaping at it from a little distance.

'It doesn't seem very French somehow,' I said as we admired the spectacle, 'reminds me of piles of whipped cream.'

Bronwyn chuckled. 'You're right, those domes are like that. And it reminds me of pictures I've seen of mosques. Still, fair play, it's very impressive.'

* * *

The next time me and Ingrid were in our room together, I said, 'Would you like to go for a coffee? You did say you'd show us round the city and there's a lot we haven't seen yet.'

She hesitated and I noticed her breathing become shallow. Then, seeming to pull herself together, she took a deep breath and slowly nodded her head. 'Give me a minute to get myself organised.'

I sat on my bed and watched as she tidied the few books and things next to her bed and put her jacket on with sharp jerky movements.

'Where shall we go?' I asked.

'How about Vincennes Zoo?' she suggested. 'We can get a bus most of the way there.'

Whether at home or in Paris, sitting upstairs in a bus always seemed like a special treat. You notice different things just because of being a few feet higher. A poorly dressed man slowly wove his way down the street, stopping from time to time to take a swig from the wine bottle in his hand. People nearby gave him a wide berth, sometimes wrinkling their noses as they walked past. In one side street we passed, a group of children were playing ring-a-ring-of-roses; most of them had no shoes. In another, a rag-and-bone man pushed a cart full of tatty bits of old clothing and bedding. We were held up at the fruit and vegetable market. Someone had driven into one of the stalls and fruit rolled this way and that across the street, as if trying to escape both the stallholder who was trying to save his wares, and the children and hungry adults who were trying to steal them. Urchins grabbed as much as possible before getting smacked in the ear for their trouble. Plump house-wives at the other stalls spent time selecting the best tomatoes or apples to put in their wicker baskets. The smell of coffee drifted up to us from a stall on the pavement, making my mouth water. And all the time the stallholders shouted out the prices for their wares.

Then I noticed that the streets didn't seem quite as busy as usual. The cafés had occasional empty seats instead of people lurking, waiting for signs that a table would become empty. And while people still walked as if always in a hurry to get to their destination, they had less people to dodge around. The buses ran faster as a result and those people who were trying to cross the streets had to be ready to jump out of their way.

'Do you think there are less people than there were?' I asked Ingrid. 'Are people scared enough to start leaving the city now?'

She looked at me sharply. 'Why on earth would I know?' she said.

'Keep your hair on,' I said, 'it was just an idle question. Is something the matter?'

She smoothed down her skirt. 'People ask too many questions,' she said, her voice so low I hardly heard her.

We rode the rest of the way in silence, broken only when we had to pay to get into the zoo.

'What animals would you like to see first?' I asked.

She gave a poor attempt at a smile. 'I don't mind, I've been here before. You can choose.'

'Let's go and see the lions then,' I said.

The weather was perfect for strolling around – warm but not too hot with wispy clouds almost stationary above us. The air was full of smells of warmed concrete, animals and popcorn from the regular stands we passed. I hadn't even been to London Zoo, so walking round Vincennes with its massive glass domed enclosures and animals I'd never even seen in picture books was amazing. I hardly knew where to look first. We stopped at the lion enclosure and leaned on the rail, finding our place between the children and parents who were crowding to see the powerful animals. Despite her earlier indifference, I saw Ingrid was captivated by the lions, her mouth curling into a gentle smile, and her shoulders relaxing.

'I love the lions,' she said, 'so strong. They know exactly what they're doing and they go for it. They don't have to worry about what anyone else thinks.'

I hadn't thought about them like that but she was right. Did she worry about what I thought of her?

'You know, Ingrid, we share a room but I don't know anything about you. Where do you come from? I'm from the outskirts of Oxford.'

'Glasgow,' she said after a long pause.

'Wow, I'd never have known, you don't sound Scottish,' I said.

'Well, that's me, we don't all speak rough in Glasgow you know. What's it to you, anyway?' Her back was rigid again and her face a mask.

I put my hand on her arm. 'I'm sorry, I don't mean to be nosey, I was just trying to be friendly.'

For a second I thought I saw the mask slip and a gentler, friendlier girl appear, but maybe I imagined it because the mask was quickly back in place. 'I'm sorry, I can be a bit short sometimes, please forgive me. I just don't like talking about the past,' she said, 'I'm more interested in the future.'

'Me, too. After this rotten war's over I suppose I'll be getting married to Edward if he's still alive.' I paused, swallowing back emotion. 'But I want to work too and not as a telephonist.'

For the first time that afternoon she looked at me properly. 'You're lucky to have options to think about. What would you like to do instead?'

I bit my lip. 'I don't know. I was assistant manager at a local cinema before the war. It was great but I'd like to do something a bit more important, more useful. I suppose I'll just have to see what's around when we get demobbed. What about you?'

'The important thing is my fam—' She stopped mid-sentence.

'Your family?'

'Nothing. I meant I need to help my family out with money, there's never enough to go round. So I'll probably go for the job that pays the most.'

I took a risk.

'Or get a sugar daddy.'

Her eyes narrowed and her jaw tightened. 'Why would you say that?' she asked, the edge back in her voice.

I could have bitten off my tongue. I didn't know her well enough to tackle her about Commander Thomas, yet I'd almost given away the fact that I knew about the affair.

'Bronwyn was joking about it the other day. Not that she's about to do it though. Still, it'd be nice to have a special person who can make you feel safe and loved as well as not having to worry about money.'

'Your Edward sounds like he be able to do that. Rich, isn't he?'

I nodded. 'That's not why I want to be with him though.'

As we walked round the zoo, she flip-flopped from being friendly to being stand-offish. It was as if she didn't trust herself to be friendly, or perhaps didn't trust anyone else with anything.

We were walking past the giraffe enclosure when something strange happened. A tall, thin, moustached man in a grey suit and a trilby hat walked towards us. He glanced at Ingrid out of the corner of his eye and I was sure they recognised each other, but both walked on without a word.

'Did you know that man?' I asked.

She stopped in her tracks and turned to face me. 'What man? There are loads of men here.'

I didn't know what to say. Challenging her would make her even more withdrawn, yet I felt already drawn into the conversation.

'The man in the grey suit who just walked past. I thought he recognised you.'

'Don't know who you mean,' she said and to my surprise she put her arm through mine and, as if she hadn't a care in the world, chatted all the way round the zoo.

8

LIFE GETS HARDER

Two days later, Amanda, Bronwyn, Mavis and I all had a morning free at the same time.

Better still, the weather continued to be fine so we decided to take a walk in the Tuileries Gardens.

On our way, we were in a little side street near the Esplanade des Invalides when we heard a girl shouting, 'Behave! Don't move! I'll clip your ears if you move an inch! You've got to come now. We'll be leaving soon.'

Turning a corner, we saw a sight that made up stop in our tracks. A girl of about ten was trying to control two younger children who were kicking her and struggling to get away, moaning that they didn't want to leave their friends and wanted to go and play. She was biting back tears.

Near them was an ancient car, half laden with what seemed like all the family's belongings, its springs groaning under the weight. A portly man came out of a nearby house carrying a big cardboard suitcase. It was so heavy he walked leaning to one side and his face was red enough to suggest he might have a heart attack any minute. He took two steps towards the car and the catch on the case suddenly broke spilling books, pictures and a Menorah onto the pavement.

'*Sacré bleu! Merde!*' he shouted, then remembered his children. 'Kids, cover your ears. Listen to me!'

He began putting the things back in the case, then noticed me and Bronwyn for the first time. 'What are you two doing, standing there watching us?'

We jumped, having been a bit mesmerised by the scene. 'Sorry, we were just passing. Can we help you?'

He grunted. 'You? Help? I don't know you from Satan. You could steal everything we have.'

Bronwyn couldn't suppress a smile. 'Come on now, man. Do we look like thieves? Your children are here to watch us. You're in a hurry. Let us load up that suitcase for you. Got an old belt or something to keep it closed?'

There was a moment's silence, then his wife who had just come out of the house said, 'Take off your belt, *bupkes*, you've got braces, your trousers won't fall down.' She grinned. 'With that stomach a belt doesn't do the job on its own.'

He glared at her but did as he was told and we were quickly drawn into helping the family move everything from the house into the car.

The wife, who told us her name was Ruth, went into the house and soon staggered out carrying a bundle of bedding that seemed bigger than her. With a grunt she spread it across the back seat. 'You can sit on this, children, you'll have a lovely soft seat.'

She turned to us and said quietly, 'And they can use the blankets to keep warm if we have to sleep in the car tonight.'

Kids from nearby houses hung around chatting to the boy and girl who still wriggled to get free.

'Hey, mister, got anything you're not taking with you?' one asked. 'I can give it to my mum or sell it.'

The father ignored him but muttered under his breath, 'Like I'd give it away. Thank goodness for pawn shops.'

It took another twenty minutes, then they declared they were done. It was impossible to get another thing in the car. It was so old it seemed like it wouldn't last till the outskirts of Paris, much less hundreds of miles further south.

'Where are you going?' I asked, picking up a dropped towel and putting it over the things in the boot.

Ruth tucked stray hair into her bun and spread her hands in an I-don't-know gesture. 'South. We don't trust the government when they say that the Nazis won't invade Paris. We're getting out. We've heard what they're doing to Jews in other countries. We've got our kids to think of.'

'Have you got people to stay with?' Bronwyn asked.

'Get in, get in,' said the father, pulling up his trousers and pushing the kids inside, 'and no whinging. I don't want to hear another word from you.' He shook our hands 'Thank you for your help. We'll keep travelling until we think we're safe enough and then rent a house. We'll be fine. Say goodbye everyone.'

A moment later, they were gone with a cloud of exhaust fumes; their lives in Paris over. But perhaps they had given themselves a future they might not otherwise have had at all if they'd got into the clutches of the Nazis.

'I wonder if they've got the right idea,' Amanda said, 'the Germans are working their way south as far as we know. What if our bosses leave it too late for us to escape?'

'I can't believe they'd do that to us. Upstairs they're still saying the Germans won't invade Paris,' Mavis said, 'but they 'ave a different leader from the last war, with 'is own ideas so I don't understand 'ow they can feel so certain.'

Amanda nodded. 'I'm going to ask when we get back – see if they will tell us anything.'

'Hard to believe anything so awful can happen on a day like this,' I said looking at the sun and clear blue sky.

By now, we'd reached the Tuileries, and were glad to rest our feet on the first bench we came to in the garden. The scent of early roses surrounded us and the breeze cooled us as the sun warmed our skin. Within a minute we all raised our faces to the sun as if worshipping an ancient god. Courting couples walked by arm in arm; mothers pushed their babies in their grand prams or shouted to their little ones to keep nearby. Elderly women, dressed in cover-all black or elegantly high-heeled, strolled past, all enjoying the respite from the city streets.

'Anyone want a fag?' Mavis asked, shaking one out of a packet and lighting up.

We shook our heads, but Amanda produced a pack of wine gums and the rest of us were soon trying to dislodge them from our teeth.

'Have you heard anything from Edward?' she asked.

I shook my head. 'You know, as each day goes by, it's harder to bring his face to mind, isn't that awful? It's only been a few months.'

Amanda prised the remains of a gum from a back tooth. 'I think it's understandable. It doesn't mean you feel any less for him. No news about prisoners of war?'

'If there is, I haven't heard it. Anyone?'

They all shook their heads, then Bronwyn said, 'Talking of that, we were going to listen in to calls to see if Ingrid is up to something. You still doing it?' She looked at me and Amanda.

Before we answered, Mavis butted in, 'You lot never told me about this, you daft sods, I 'ear all sorts up there.' She pointed upwards as if the office she worked in were above us.

I could have slapped myself for not thinking of that. 'Well, you know that we're always being told to watch what we say, keep an eye out for spies—'

'Fifth columnists,' she interrupted.

'That's right. We wondered if Ingrid was up to something. She's very secretive and sometimes the things she says to one of us contradicts what she says to another. It's like she can't remember her lies.'

Bronwyn reached for another sweet, taking her time to choose her favourite colour. 'Or maybe she's just a habitual liar, I've come across plenty of them in Swansea, I can tell you. Half of my family for a start.'

Mavis took another drag of her Gitane. 'You know she's 'aving it off with Commander Thomas, I suppose?' she said, blowing the bitter smoke away from us.

We all gaped at her. 'We guessed, but what... how do you know?'

She raised an eyebrow. 'Got eyes and ears, ain't I? Plain as the nose on your face. Always sneaking off together, them two, or giving each other little glances they think the rest of us can't see. I even saw 'em one day going into a little hotel in some side street when I was out for a walk.'

Bronwyn whistled. 'What it is, see, she might be getting him to tell her all secret stuff while he's feeling randy. You know what happens to men's brains when their other parts take over.'

Amanda laughed. 'It's not like you to be so delicate about it, Bronwyn!'

'But if she's getting secrets, she must be passing them on somehow,' I said. 'Surely she wouldn't use the telephones at work. Should we report this?'

Mavis snickered. 'Who would you report it to? Commander Thomas? I don't think so, and none of the others would dare do anything against him, he's their boss.'

We were silent for a minute waiting for a courting couple to walk past so we wouldn't be overheard.

'It's up to us then,' Amanda said, 'we have to turn spies ourselves to see what she's up to.'

'What, follow her and that?' Mavis asked.

'Yes, if we have to. You read about people doing that all the time in detective novels.'

'Surely we'll need disguises,' I said, 'she'll soon spot us otherwise. Anyone got a wig?'

'How about we get some hats,' Bronwyn said, 'we can stop at the flea market on the way back today...'

'And buy 'ats full of fleas...' Mavis said.

'Good point, we'll check carefully to make sure there are no fleas. Then we can carry umbrellas. Good if it rains, and we can always pretend they're parasols if the sun is hot.'

'Or a newspaper, so if she turns around, we can lean against a wall and pretend to read.'

'What do we do if she stops?' Mavis asked, stubbing out her Gitane, and reaching for a sweet.

Amanda slapped her hand. 'In the book I'm reading, the private eye following the baddie carries on walking, right past them, then hides in a shop or round the corner of the building until the baddie walks past. Then he carries on following him. I'm sure we can do that. Has anyone got any other ideas?'

I thought for a minute. 'It's probably nothing, but I've noticed she always has a little notebook with her. Says it's where she jots down poems or anything else that comes into her head. I wonder if she can be making notes in it?'

Amanda raised her eyebrows. 'Does she guard it with her life?'

'Well, she has it with her most of the time, but not religiously. I've seen her leave it on her bed when she goes to the bathroom. Must admit, I've never looked in it.'

Bronwyn clapped her hands. 'She wouldn't worry, would she? She'd be writing in code for sure.' She looked at her watch. 'If we're going to have time to follow someone, we'd better head back before too long. Got to have time for a coffee on the way.'

Agreeing to meet back home, we split into pairs to practise our sleuthing. Mavis and I followed a smart woman. Dressed elegantly in dark blue, with a leather clutch bag and high heel shoes, we decided she probably wouldn't walk too fast for us to keep up with. We thought we were doing well, dodging in and out of shop doorways, walking past her on one occasion, and peering at her reflection in shop windows when we had to stop. But our success was short lived because she went into a doorway and didn't reappear. We hung around for ten minutes trying to seem inconspicuous, but when she didn't come out, we called it a day.

'I'm surprised she didn't hear our giggles,' Mavis said, 'At least if we're following Ingrid on our own that won't be a danger.'

If only she'd been right.

9

A WORRYING DEVELOPMENT

I continued to write to Edward every week, although I hadn't heard a word from him. I even tried writing to his mother again, asking if she had any news. It took her two weeks to reply which was a terse 'no news'. Every night I said a prayer for him, and as I lay in bed I tried hard to banish all pictures of him being tortured, or starving or being made to do awful back-breaking work – or dead.

Then, one Wednesday when I was on duty, headset in place, things changed. Sorting the incoming mail was one of Mavis's tasks and she knew I'd been waiting for a letter.

'Got something for you,' she said, trying not to smile.

'Is it a letter from my mum?' I asked. 'Hand it over.'

She produced the letter from behind her back like a magician pulling a rabbit out of a hat. She went to hand it over, then snatched it back at the last minute when I held out my hand for it. She thought it was a great game. This happened twice and I was ready to kill her. I transferred two calls while she was messing about. I could tell the letter wasn't from home, the envelope was completely different. It had to be from Edward. In the end, I ripped the headset off and chased her, grabbing the letter she was trying to hold over her head.

'Sorry,' she said, laughing so much she could hardly speak, ''ard to resist teasing you.'

Amanda was the other person on duty and she saw what was happening. 'Take it to the Ladies' to read,' she said, 'I'll cover for you.'

Slapping Mavis as I walked past, I ran to the toilet hugging the letter to my heart. The envelope was grubby, with fingerprints and muddy smears here and there. It also seemed as if it had been opened and poorly stuck back down. But I recognised Edward's handwriting and gently stroked it with my fingers. I opened the envelop carefully, fearful of tearing any part of it. I took out the letter with trembling hands, tears already threatening to spill. It said:

My dear Lily,

I have received a few letters from you although I realise from reading them that you have written more that haven't arrived. I read and reread your words until I fear the paper will disintegrate. You will never know how much they mean to me. Hearing about your everyday life is such a balm, reminding me that there is life outside where I am now.

You may know that I am a prisoner of war in Plaszow, Poland, although we have been moved around three different camps already. Mother sends Red Cross parcels regularly, although often the guards help themselves before we get them. I hope that you and Mother are keeping in touch. I like to think that one good thing to come from being captured is that you two will find something in common and become more friendly. If she hadn't already done so, she will learn to love you like the daughter she never had.

We are worked hard here, although I cannot say doing what. We are treated okay, although I XXXXXXX it brings.

But we keep our spirits up and enjoy the comradeship that has grown between us.

Remember the picnic by the stream where you splashed me? It was a beautiful warm day but the water was cold enough to take my breath away. We lay in the sun after our picnic and you snuggled your head on my chest. It was the most wonderful feeling, and I realised that we were meant for each other.

I will write again when I'm allowed to and hope that you are still enjoying your work wherever you are. I was so pleased to hear you have some familiar friends to keep you company.

I can't wait until we are together again and can begin planning our wedding day.

Yours, with love,

Your devoted fiancé, Edward

I tried and tried to see the words that had been crossed out, but without luck. The other girls had received letters similarly hacked about from their brothers who were fighting. The main thing was, he was alive. Or at least he was when the letter was written a month before. And he still loved me; he still loved me. Just reading his letter brought his face, which had been fading from my mind, back into sharp focus. I had a sudden powerful surge of longing, to be in his arms, to feel secure, to feel the world was a safe place to be.

I spent so long day-dreaming there, in the Ladies', that Mavis came and knocked on the door. 'Are you okay?' she asked. 'It isn't bad news, is it?'

I unlocked the cubical and gave her watery smile. 'No, everything's fine. He's alive!' And I walked out into the hand-wash area and spun round like a lunatic, grinning until the muscles in my face started to ache.

* * *

A few days later, Ingrid took over my headset at the end of my shift. I noticed that, unusually, she didn't have her little book with her. I stood by the door until I saw her beginning to take calls then decided to do some sleuthing. Perhaps there would be some evidence in her little book.

Not the brightest of rooms at the best of times, our bedroom was already in darkness as I crossed the hall and stood at the threshold. Although the room was so familiar to me after all these weeks as the place nearest to one I called home, I was again aware of how little I knew of my room-mate. Despite being so close to each other day and night, I still didn't know her well. So, as I stood there, about to search her side of the room for her book, it was as if the belongings I was about to rummage in were those of a stranger. I pulled the light switch cord on the light fitting in the middle of the room and thought about where to start.

The dressing table was one we both used and I knew it wouldn't be there because I'd have seen it before. I started on her bedside cabinet where an ashtray with half a dozen dog-ends sat on a small pile of Paris street maps. There was a handwritten copy of her duty rota, half folded, tucked under a small glass jar that held some small items of jewellery. The drawer beneath contained only a collection of underwear and a pair of apparently well used and darned stockings. I took care not to move anything and felt like a real spy for a minute.

Opening the cabinet door beneath, revealed a tall box of cheap French talcum powder; a tube of antiseptic cream; a small brown bottle of pills; two or three folded white hankies, and, right at the back, four condoms. I suddenly felt the urge to snigger at this last finding until the awful thought occurred to me that the user of these might be Commander Thomas himself and, instead, I shuddered in mild disgust. I stood and turned to the alcove at the end of her bed and the pitiful collection of uniforms and odd bits of her civilian clothes that hung there on a rail. A quick pat of the pockets showed the book wasn't there.

I turned back to the bed and, without thinking, tugged at the eiderdown. The book, caught in its folds, flew from the bed and fell with a flutter of pages into the floor at my feet. Guiltily, as if she could hear the noise from the duty room, I noticed that the brown paper covering was starting to come away and I wondered if this was my doing in dropping it to the floor. I inspected the flap of paper that had come loose and saw where it become unglued on the inside of the front cover. I also saw that Ingrid's name was written in blue pen on the first fly leaf 'Ingrid Foster'. But there, on the back of the front cover and until now hidden by the brown paper was another inscription in a different hand. *'Zu unserer süßen tochter*. Ingrid Abelsdor. Matty und Papa'. I felt the hair on the back of my neck prickle and for a moment felt light-headed. I retreated to my own bed and sat heavily wondering what on earth I had found. My first instinct was to lick the glued seams and press them together again to hide what I had seen. No sooner had I done this than I felt another urge to pull the paper back again to reassure myself that I had, in fact, seen what I thought I had.

Pull yourself together, I told myself, *you've done nothing wrong*. But I grabbed a pen and paper and copied the words in case I should ever need them.

I began searching my mind for what I did know about Ingrid. She gave very little away to anyone and nobody knew that much about her, that much was clear. She was having an affair with a man more than twice her years without ever professing any fondness for him. She rarely went out with the other ATS girls in her spare time, yet seldom went straight back to her room either. So where did she go? I stood, straightened my tunic, turned off the light and stood in the darkened door way. My mind was in such a whirl it was impossible to settle, so I decided to go for a walk before turning in for the night. But first, I returned the book to where I'd found it.

It was never dark in Paris despite the blackout regulations. Narrow strips of light seeped through the doorways of cafés and nightclubs, and reflected the white paint on the road crossings and the white capes worn by traffic gendarmes. The street lights were fitted with dimmers and the posts had a protective covering in case drivers crashed into them. As I walked through a little square I thought how different it was by moonlight. Then the moon properly appeared from behind a cloud, casting shadows that emphasised features I'd never noticed in daylight which seemed somehow threatening. The church on one side of the square had gargoyles where the roof and walls met. The shadows made their horns and noses elongated as if they might come alive at any moment. In my troubled mental state, I imagined German soldiers marching through – the ring of their jackboots echoing aggressively round the old walls.

I walked through the square and back to the bigger streets which felt safer. Although not crowded, couples strolled arm in arm here and there, people walked their dogs, and solitary walkers hurried to their destinations. I'd already learned to rely on my night-sight to avoid falling over objects on the pavement or trip at kerbs, so my mind was free to wander. Should I report what I knew of Ingrid? Did the authorities know that she was really German? Come to that, she might have a German name but have been born in England. Where would her loyalties lie?

Stopping to pet a German shepherd and exchange a brief word

with its owner, brought me back to reality, but my doubts soon crept back in. If I reported her, presumably Commander Thomas would be the most senior person who'd have to know about it within our building. Would his lust overcome his concern for the safety of Britain, or would he be willing to turn Ingrid in? I wished my brain would turn off, so I could go to bed and get a good night's sleep before my early shift next day.

The welcome sound of a Maurice Chevalier song broke through my troubled thoughts and I did something I'd never done before. I went into a bar late in the evening on my own. It was busy, but not noisy, with a strong smell of coffee and Gitanes. A few men eyed me up when I entered, but getting no response, carried on with their conversation. Feeling very daring, I ordered a cognac and sat in a corner sipping it slowly. Gradually, the warmth of the alcohol eased my tension and I decided to think about other things. I remembered life at home with Mum, and hoped she would ditch that slimy boyfriend soon. I thought back to the letter I'd received from Jean who was still enjoying her nursing and courting a doctor. But most of all I thought about Edward and the wonderful times we'd had together. Within half an hour, I felt relaxed enough to head back home. I double-checked that I'd left all Ingrid's things as they were, cleaned my teeth and fell in bed, asleep within minutes.

The next day we heard that Amiens had fallen to the Germans and that their troops had crossed the Meuse River. It seemed that every day the news got worse, and the Germans got nearer and nearer to Paris.

Marie-Claude at the soup kitchen soon noticed that there were fewer and fewer Jews queuing for food each day. 'They may be gone, but we've got all the refugees from Belgium and Holland instead,' she said, 'will this never end? How are we going to get enough food to feed everyone?'

Sure enough the couple I'd spoken to at the flea market no longer came for food, and I was sorry to miss them. I silently wished them a safe journey to wherever they'd chosen to go.

In the office, there was little talk of anything but the German advances. Accurate information was always hard to come by, but I heard from the refugees at the soup kitchen what they'd seen and passed on what I knew. None of it was good.

Bronwyn came to my room one evening when Ingrid was out. 'Where's she gone?' she asked, nodding at Ingrid's empty bed.

I shrugged. 'No idea. She never says where she's going. Have you noticed she seems really unhappy? Dark rings round her eyes and she jumps a mile at every loud sound.'

Bronwyn sat next to me on the bed. 'That's what I came to see you about. I did a stint following her yesterday. She went into a small hotel with the boss. I sat in a café opposite pretending to read the paper. Just about to give up, I was, when they came out. Must have been an hour later. He came out first, checked up and down the street, then strode away without a care in the world. I waited, then about five minutes later she came out.

'Not being funny or nothing, but she looked miserable as sin,' Bronwyn said.

'Any idea why?' I asked.

It was her turn to shrug. 'No idea. I wonder if she's regretting getting together with him. Perhaps he hits her or something.'

We sat for a few more minutes throwing around ideas for the cause of Ingrid's misery but had no evidence to go on and could hardly ask her.

'I had one more bit of news,' Bronwyn said, 'I heard we'll be among the last to go if the Germans invade Paris.'

I felt the blood drain from my face. 'Are you joking?'

'No, Mrs Perkins said that they need to keep communications open until the last minute.'

I took her hand. 'Oh my goodness, Bronwyn. Let's pray they get their timing right or we're done for.'

Summer was progressing as Bronwyn and I sat outside a café on the Champs-Élysées. The horse chestnut trees were vibrant. 'The smell of these trees reminds me of you-know-what,' Bronwyn said.

'You-know-what? What do you mean?'

'A bit of the other.' She put her head closer to mine and whispered, 'Sex.'

I was so stunned I didn't know how to reply, and sat there feeling stupid.

'I keep forgetting your lack of knowledge. Ignore me,' Bronwyn said, 'let's talk about something else. You know we have to pay extra to sit in the front row like this. Mind you, it's a good opportunity to see and be seen.'

Still bemused, I looked down at our none-too-smart clothes and decided we had no reason to want to be seen. But it was great having a bird's-eye view of the people walking by. Better to watch them than to take in the newspaper headlines we saw in the newsagent stand next to our café. The war news was still all doom and gloom. Hundreds of thousands of people fleeing not only from northern France but from Belgium and Holland. All trying to get away from the unstoppable German army. Every day we saw more of them passing through Paris. They obviously didn't have confidence that the French government would stop the Germans invading the capital city.

Bronwyn and I watched a family go by, their smart car laden with their belongings. The parents looked harassed and the children were crying.

'I wonder where they've come from?' Bronwyn asked. 'I wonder where they'll end up?'

We lapsed into silence again, then returned to our most common topic of conversation. Would we get out of Paris in time if the Nazis invaded? We'd go round and round in circles, tormenting ourselves because we didn't know the answer. We knew we'd be among the last British forces people to leave the city, because communication was vital, but how late would they leave it?

'Let's talk about something more cheerful,' Bronwyn said. 'Didn't you get a letter this morning? Was it from Edward?'

'No, it was from my mum and there was fantastic news. She's dumped that awful bloke she was seeing. The one who tried to get fresh with me.'

Bronwyn pulled a face. 'He was a bad 'un for sure. Did she say what made her see the light?'

'Someone told her he was two-timing her, seeing another woman from the street where he lived. Worse, he'd been spotted trying to touch up the woman's daughter who was only thirteen.'

She groaned. 'Oh God, I hope someone cuts off his bits – disgusting man. I don't know how they can live with themselves.'

We were making ourselves depressed again, and gloomily looking round when Bronwyn suddenly perked up. 'Hey! There's Ingrid. Let's follow her. It shouldn't be too difficult; she's wearing her favourite yellow jumper.' Ingrid was hurrying along the street, confidently, as if she knew her way by heart.

We threw some francs on the table and followed her from the other side of the road.

It was much easier to follow her than we expected. Ingrid was focused on where she was going, and never glanced our way. We simply had to dodge round other pedestrians, prams, dogs and excitable children. We were feeling very smug and even giggling a bit at our spying skills when it all went wrong.

Without warning, Ingrid went into a Metro station.

'Damn, we'll lose her!' Bronwyn cried.

Narrowly avoiding cars, bicycles and horse drawn carts, we ran across the road after her. Not knowing where she was going we bought tickets to the end of the line, then hurried on.

Following Ingrid was harder now. We were walking along the same passageways, but there were enough people around for us to always stay back out of sight. More than once we gave silent thanks for that yellow sweater.

Ingrid walked onto the platform, and stood without any sign of being aware of us. We held back, and when she got on the train, waited until the last minute and then ran into another carriage just before the doors closed.

I could hardly speak, I was so out of breath, yet we'd only hurried about five feet. My heart was thumping and I felt it might choke me any minute. Bronwyn saw my distress. 'Take a few deep breaths, *cariad*,' she said.

She was right, it did help. 'How can I be so out of breath?' I asked.

She grinned. 'Not being funny, but it's just tension. Following her was fun, but it might be really serious.'

I nodded. 'And who knows what we're going to find.'

At each station we peered through the window to see if Ingrid was getting off, but she stayed on until Place de la Bastille. Darting around like frightened fish, we dodged behind people as we got off, looking under arms and round shoulders to keep that yellow in sight.

The Metro was beautiful, a style I'd learned was art nouveau, with a graceful arch over the entrance and exit with lots of panes of glass at the top, and the curved shape continuing down the side, making another elegant arch.

Bronwyn nudged me. 'Stop gaping and keep your mind on the

job. Come on!' She yanked me by the arm and we followed Ingrid down a nearby street. It was narrow with pavements either side and cobbles between. Three storey houses flanked either side. It was easy to see that some were still occupied by a single person, the outside well cared for and sometimes having window boxes. Others were divided up into rooms or apartments where washing hung out of windows or people sat on steps passing the time chatting to neighbours.

There were fewer people about so it got harder to follow Ingrid without being seen. We stayed well back and were relieved when she turned into another street that was busier with more places to hide. It was a mixture of small shops, such as greengrocers, with stalls outside, and houses obviously split into smaller dwellings. Children ran around, often barefoot, playing kiss/chase causing a lot of laughs and cries of pretend disgust. Old ladies dressed in black sat outside their doors, knitting; preparing vegetables, darning; or just watching the world go by. A group of men played boules in an alleyway, their backs bent from years of hard work, their flat caps greasy and well worn.

Another fifty yards and Ingrid turned abruptly into an alleyway and we just managed to catch sight of her disappearing into a doorway about halfway down. We stood in the entrance to the alley wondering what to do. There were a few people about, more children playing and occasional people walking through.

'How can we find where she is?' I asked Bronwyn. 'We know which door, but not where she is in the building. And people will see us snooping.'

She put her hands on her hips, a gesture I'd seen her do before when she wanted to spring into action or get her point across forcefully. 'I'm not going to lie to you. It's difficult, but here's what we can do. Let's pretend we're searching for a house and walk up and down the alley checking the numbers. Then if anyone challenges us we can tell them that's what we're doing.'

I bit my lip. 'But what if Ingrid sees us?'

She shook her head. 'Whatever we do, that's a danger. We either give it a try or give up. What do you think?'

I felt my insides getting wobbly at the thought of trying her suggestion. She nudged me hard. 'Come on, what's the worst that can happen? She's not going to shoot us, is she?'

I wasn't sure that helped. If she really was a spy she could have a gun for all we knew. So might whoever she was meeting.

Taking a deep breath, I said, 'Come on, just once up and down though, or we'll be too suspicious.'

We said a polite *'Bonjour'* to people we passed and made a big play of looking at numbers. Probably too big a play. When we got to the building where Ingrid was we slowed down immediately before we got to the window. It was open and we heard voices.

'That's her,' Bronwyn whispered, 'but I can't quite make out what she's saying.'

I pressed my ear as near to the window as I dared and listened for a minute. Then I turned to Bronwyn, my eyes big as the moon. 'She's talking German!' I whispered.

Her jaw dropped and her eyes questioned mine. I nodded. 'She is!'

Bronwyn grabbed my hand and pulled me back the way we'd come. 'Come on, let's get out of here!' she hissed.

You'd have thought a platoon of German soldiers were on our heels; we ran so fast from that building, not stopping for breath until we turned the corner. Even then we walked so quickly we had no breath to speak. We made sure to walk in the opposite direction from the one we'd come, in case Ingrid made her way back home. The weather was turning; dark, threatening storm clouds headed towards Paris, bringing a chilly wind that made us hug ourselves as we hurried along.

Ten minutes later we came to a busy street and dived into a café. It was half empty but so full of cigarette smoke it was almost like walking through fog.

Baguettes with cheese or ham were stacked on the counter ready for the next mealtime rush. No sitting at the front table on the pavement for us this time. We sat as far back inside as possible, as if Ingrid would walk past any minute and see us. We ordered coffees and took them with us to our table.

'She's got to be a spy,' I said when we had checked that no one was near enough to hear us.

Bronwyn nodded, her face like stone. 'It does look like it, but perhaps we shouldn't jump to conclusions. Amanda speaks German. It's just possible that Ingrid learned to speak German as a child and has some friends here. We don't have any evidence.'

She was right. There was nothing to tie her to spying, just our suspicions and some odd behaviour. If we went to Mrs Perkins with that, she'd just laugh at us. And with Ingrid's relationship with Commander Thomas an issue, we were even less likely to be taken seriously.

'It's odd that she hardly tells us a thing about herself,' I said.

Bronwyn nodded. 'Fair do. Most of us just mention things about our home from time to time. It's like getting blood out of a stone trying to get anything out of her. Perhaps she's just a private person.'

I took a sip of the coffee; it was so hot it burned my tongue. 'Maybe. We had some neighbours once who never told you a thing. If one of them had died we'd never have known.'

Bronwyn nodded. 'I know some families have a rule that you don't talk about what goes on in the house outside of the house. Not much choice where we always lived. We either shared rooms with other families or the walls were so thin you heard everything that went on. More than you wanted, often.'

The following morning Ingrid went out early, creeping out of bed before I was normally awake if it wasn't my shift. I threw on some clothes and hurried after her, wishing I'd had time to wash my face and brush my hair. Luck was on my side; some people in one of the other flats were having a furious row, throwing things at each other. The racket they made covered my footsteps as I rushed down the stairs after her, tucking my blouse in my skirt.

She walked quickly, with a purpose, and I had to frequently hide in doorways or duck behind buses when she slowed or looked like turning round. Paris was only just waking up. Milk floats trundled noisily though the streets; dog walkers waited impatiently for their dogs to do their business or sniff a wall or tree; a coal lorry was delivering its load into a grand house; and cafés were doing a roaring trade selling tiny cups of coffee to early workers who drank it standing up then hurried on their way. Further on, the delicious smell of fresh bread drifted behind people who carried their baguettes under their arms.

Ingrid was heading into an area I didn't know and I started to worry about getting lost and not being able to find my way back. She went inside a synagogue. At least, I guessed that was what it was from the big Star of David over the door. I didn't dare go in because I had no idea if there would be anywhere to hide. Instead, I crouched behind a low wall opposite. I checked my watch regularly. Maybe, I thought, she was going to a service. I wondered how long synagogue services lasted. What if it was an hour? I was on duty at midday, just four hours away.

Ten minutes later, my worries proved unfounded because she

came out and continued walking in the same direction. She'd never mentioned being religious before, or indeed being Jewish, so I was surprised that she'd gone to a synagogue. Half an hour later, I was even more surprised when she went inside a Catholic church. I had no idea what the inside of a synagogue was like, but knew that there would be hiding places inside a church as long as I was careful. So, I waited a minute or two then followed her in. She was just dipping her hand into the holy water in the special basin a little way inside the door. Then she crossed herself and walked halfway down the church. She went into one of the pews and knelt down to pray. I watched her silently and as soon as she made to stand up, hurried outside and hid round a corner. She soon appeared and continued on her way.

Was she making her peace with her God? Perhaps she had one Jewish parent and one Catholic one and had regularly gone to both places of worship. Was she asking the Deity for support? Hoping for a few minutes' peace? I'd never know.

The morning had turned warm, but gusty winds blew my hair around my face and I had to keep pushing it away. Sometimes I'd see people walking along normally, then be caught by a sudden gust of wind and almost fall as they were thrown forward, their clothes ballooning around them, then the wind would drop, they'd straighten up and carry on as before.

We walked a long way north until we were almost on the banks of the Seine. With aching feet I wondered if Ingrid would ever stop, so I was relieved when she turned off the road. There was a big notice showing it was the Cimetière des Chiens – the pet cemetery. I'd never seen it before or even heard of it. It was a grand place with wrought iron gates attached to a large stone arch; elegant, imposing. Either side were smaller arches. I'd never seen a cemetery for people half as impressive.

The cemetery was enormous, stretching either way as far as the eye could see.

Ingrid walked confidently and clearly knew where she was going, never deviating or hesitating. It made it easy to follow her, although I kept near headstones big enough to hide behind. There were plenty of them. I was amazed that pet owners lavished so much care and money on the final resting place of their dog or cat. I spotted a headstone for the old canine film star, Rin Tin Tin. Underneath his name, it said '*La Grande Vedette du Cinema*'. Plenty of owners seemed to give their pets more lavish headstones than many people got where I lived.

Eventually, Ingrid stopped at one of the more modest graves. It was about eighteen inches high and had a stone dog kennel on a flat platform. If the dog's name had been inscribed over the door, it was worn away with time and weather. Moss on the roof showed that the dog's owners hadn't visited for a long time and were probably also in heaven. I hoped they were reunited there if such a place existed. Ingrid reached into the kennel and took out an envelope. She quickly scanned the contents, then put it in her bag, taking out another which she put inside the kennel.

Crouching, I peered from behind a headstone, and just as well, because she suddenly spun on her heel and started to retrace her steps. But now her steps were slower, halting, and tears were flowing down her cheeks. She brushed them away and I heard her say 'Stupid!' to herself. Then, as if she was unable to contain it any longer, she let out a loud sob, took out her hankie and used it to muffle the sound of her weeping.

I hid until she'd gone, debating whether to follow her, but decided she would probably go back home. I was left with a dilemma. Should I go and read the note? What if whoever was picking it up arrived? If they saw me, it was likely they would be aggressive, after all, whoever it was, was a spy. I stood for a couple of minutes, dithering, then realised that the longer I waited, the more likely it was that the spy would appear. Almost tiptoeing, I hurried over to the grave and snatched the envelope, managing to open it without ripping it. With shaking hands I took out the sheet of paper and opened it. My heart sank when I saw that the message was written in German.

There was no mistaking now. Ingrid was definitely spying for the Nazis.

I took the message and envelope and hid behind a tree some distance from the grave. Getting notepaper and a pencil out of my bag, I copied the message, double-checking each letter – I wouldn't have known if I'd made a mistake because I didn't understand a word.

I heard footsteps, and my heart jumped and beat so loud I felt sure anyone within fifty feet would hear it. Trying to breathe normally, I peered round the tree. It was an elderly lady carrying a small bunch of flowers tied with a blue ribbon. Before she reached me, she turned left and walked towards a different part of the cemetery. Letting out a long sigh, I put the message back in the envelope, and resealed it as best I could. I looked around and, feeling like a spy in *The Thirty Nine Steps*, crept around checking every few seconds that there was no one following me.

Back at the grave dog kennel, I tried without success to remember exactly where Ingrid had left the envelope. In the end I just put it to one side so it would be out of sight. I would need a lot of training if I was ever going to be a proper spy. But I had the sense to walk back towards the gates along a parallel path. I hadn't gone a hundred yards when a huge, burly man with straggly blond hair walked towards the kennel grave. Creeping back, I watched him, my knees feeling as if they would give way any moment. He glanced around and, seeing no one, took the envelope, hastily shoved it in his pocket and retraced his steps.

I considered following him, but he walked much faster than I could. In any case, if he spotted me I might be in real danger. He didn't seem like a man you'd want to cross swords with. I waited ten minutes, then cautiously left the cemetery and headed back home.

Shaking, I made my way out of the cemetery and stopped at the first café for a coffee and croissant. My mind was all over the place wondering what to do. But resting my sore feet and having the coffee and food eventually got my brain in gear. I'd ask Amanda to translate the message. Then, assuming it was incriminating, we'd go to see Mrs Perkins.

I was putting a few centimes down for a tip when a dreadful thought came into my mind. Was it possible Amanda was a spy? She spoke German, and you heard about wealthy people supporting Hitler. As I walked slowly back, I thought back over all the conversations I'd had with her since we started training together. By the time I was back at the office, I realised I'd been worrying for nothing.

Because of our shifts, it was several hours before I could talk to Amanda without anyone overhearing. The whole time I was on edge, and kept clutching the copy of the note as if it might disappear out of my bag. When she finished her shift, I went to her bedroom.

'Fancy a drink before you turn in?' I asked.

She yawned and eased off her shoes. 'I was thinking of an early night, to be honest.'

Checking no one was looking, I took hold of her arm, 'Yes, you do fancy a drink, that's good.' I gestured over my shoulder towards the door and she got the message.

Going over to her cupboard, she got out a different pair of shoes, put on a coat and followed me out of the flat.

'Are we going to Henri's?' she asked, as we walked down the stairs.

'No, somewhere quieter. Let's find the emptiest bar.'

It didn't take long. Once we got off the main road, smaller bars were emptier and mostly occupied by locals. We chose a small bar two streets away. Getting a glass of red wine each we sat as far away as possible from other people. Most of them seemed too old to have good hearing anyway, but we were trained to be cautious.

'*Salute!*' Amanda said, and we clinked glasses. She dropped her voice. 'Now, what's this about?'

I explained about following Ingrid and got out the copy of the letter she had left. 'Can you translate this? I hope I've copied it out right.'

She took the piece of paper from me as if it might blow up in her hand. Taking a deep breath, she unfolded it and started reading. She read it three times without comment, the little frown lines between her eyes getting deeper, then she gripped my arm tightly.

'This is information about British troop movements,' she said, 'highly classified. It would be of great help to the German army. She must be getting it from Commander Thomas. What a stupid man he must be.'

My shoulders slumped and I let out a low whistle. 'Blimey, Amanda, what are we going to do?'

'I'd love to know why she does it,' Amanda said, 'we have all noticed how unhappy she seems, it makes you wonder if she wants to be a...' She stopped herself. 'Wants to do what she's doing.' Now she peered around too.

I frowned. 'But why else would she do it?'

'Didn't you say you'd seen her go into a synagogue? I wonder if she is part Jewish, if you can be part Jewish. Not sure if you can. Perhaps she has family who are in danger.'

We put our heads closer together so that we could speak even more quietly. 'And she's being blackmailed, you mean?' I said.

'Who knows? But it's possible. But whatever it is, we can't let it go on. We need to talk to Bronwyn and Mavis before we do anything, see if they have anything else to add. What shift are you on tomorrow?'

We worked out that all four of us would be free from midday for two hours. Then we sat nursing our little glasses of wine, too worried to speak much. After half an hour, we gave up trying to cheer ourselves up and went back to the flat.

The next day was cloudy and dull, with occasional spits of rain. The four of us huddled under our umbrellas and made our way back to the café Amanda and I had been in the night before. It was packed. We hadn't taken into account that it was lunchtime, so locals were there having coffee and their cheese baguettes.

'It's going to be the same everywhere,' I said, 'where can we chat?'

We ended up in a beautiful little-used church with a wonderful rose window and unusual Stations of the Cross paintings around the walls. We worried about our voices echoing, but there was no one else in there and we kept a careful eye on the door. We huddled tight, our heads close together, and spoke in low voices.

Amanda and I told Mavis and Bronwyn all we had found out.

'Now, after,' said Bronwyn, 'we've got to tell Mrs Perkins.'

'What if she doesn't do anything because of Commander Thomas?' Mavis asked.

'What if she does, and he doesn't do anything?' I said. 'He might make trouble for us.'

'Well, if he tries that, Mrs Perkins will back us up, after all, we'll have told her. Mind you, he could make trouble for her, too.'

Mavis spoke up. 'I've seen a lot of Commander Thomas. He thinks with 'is you-know-what a lot of the time; us girls 'ave to stay out of the way of 'is wandering hands. But 'e never seems to mind – it's like it's a fun sport for him. Doesn't seem to hold a grudge if we reject him.'

We were all quiet for a minute, then I spoke. 'That may be true, Mavis, but this is a bit different. He'll be in big trouble for giving away secrets.'

In unison, we all sat back. My mind was a whirl, full of questions and doubts. Would Commander Thomas cause trouble? Would he get court-martialled? Apart from his wandering hands, people seemed to have a good opinion of him. If he were court-martialled who would be our new boss?

Amanda broke into my thoughts. 'One big issue is when we can get Mrs Perkins on her own to tell her.'

I thought for a minute. 'Ingrid is on duty this evening, we can tell her then.'

'What if Mrs Perkins is on duty herself?' Mavis asked.

'Even if she is, she goes to her office sometimes. Mind you, it would probably be better if Ingrid was out, but we have no way of knowing when that would be.'

'We can't delay, girls,' Bronwyn said. 'Who knows what other information she's passing on. Let's go back now and see if either of them are in.'

'Mrs Perkins is on duty now,' Mavis said. 'I saw the rota.'

'Right,' Bronwyn said, all action, 'it's like this. One of us goes and tries to get her. If Ingrid is around, we get her to come here or go somewhere else in the building.'

'I know where,' Mavis said, getting out her Gitanes, 'there's the empty room next to the Ladies'. It's got old desks and stuff in it. We could get 'er there.'

She lit up and took a big drag of her cigarette. 'Come on, let's go.'

* * *

I told Mrs Perkins the four of us needed to see her, and we agreed a time when she was free. She seemed surprised, but didn't argue. Amanda, Mavis, Bronwyn and me went ahead to the quiet bar we'd found before. It wasn't lunchtime, so the place was pretty empty. We needn't have worried too much about 'walls have ears' though because we all felt so down we didn't say much, but just sat staring into our drinks.

'I'm not being funny or nothing,' Bronwyn eventually said, 'but what if we're wrong? We'll look pretty stupid.'

'Or crazy,' Mavis said.

'Or vindictive,' Amanda chipped in.

'How much evidence do you want?' I said, keeping my voice low, 'we've got more than enough for anyone to take us seriously.' I checked the time. 'Come on, girls, finish your drinks. Time for our appointment.'

* * *

The small room was strangely quiet despite me and four others in it. Traffic noises were muted, as well as the shout of the newspaper-seller and the call of the rag-and-bone man. A thick blanket of concentration and fear insulated us.

'Are you absolutely certain of all this, girls?' Mrs Perkins said, her voice more stern than I had ever heard it. 'These are very serious accusations against Ingrid and a senior officer.'

While never a smiley woman, her face was often kind but now

it was as steely grey as her hair. She unbuttoned her jacket, then buttoned it up again.

I spoke for all of us. 'We can't say for sure she is a spy, but everything we have told you is true.' I reached in my pocket and took out the note I'd found in the dog kennel gravestone. 'Here, this is the note. Amanda has written the translation underneath.'

Mrs Perkins took it from me as if it carried a contagious disease. 'Is this the actual note?'

I shook my head, 'No, I don't know if I did the right thing, but I thought it safer to copy the note and put the original back where it was.'

She studied the paper again. 'I don't speak much German, but I'm sure you are accurate in your translation, Amanda. This is serious, very serious. I need to have time to think what to do. Can I ask you girls to keep this to yourself?'

We all nodded.

'Absolute silence on the matter. Do not give away to the people concerned that you have any suspicions. Act normally at all times. But be assured, I will be taking some action to deal with this. I may not be able to tell you what it is. You'll just have to trust me. Do you understand?'

'Yes, Mrs Perkins.' We spoke in unison like children speaking to their teacher.

'Off you go then, and thank you for bringing this to my attention. I appreciate it can't have been easy for you.'

I glanced back as we filed out of the room. Mrs Perkins was sitting with her head in her hands, a picture of absolute despair.

I was glad that Ingrid was out that evening, and went to bed early to avoid having to talk to her. Could she really be a spy? Although she was a private sort of person, I didn't dislike her, in fact if anything I found myself feeling sorry for her; she seemed so unhappy. But then I thought back to all the spy stories I'd read and one or two I'd heard about in the news. Maybe her behaviour was all a cover. Smarter people than me had been fooled by spies, sometimes for years and years. All this was relentlessly whirling in my brain when I heard Ingrid come in. But instead of saying good-night as I normally would, I lay pretending to be asleep, trying hard to keep my breathing even. Irrationally, I suddenly wondered if she'd hurt me if she found out what we'd done. I kept awake until I was sure she was asleep, before I let myself relax enough to fall asleep myself.

Next morning, Mrs Perkins was nowhere to be seen. When I asked around, I was told she had booked a day's leave. I managed to catch a few words with Mavis when she delivered the post.

'Heard anything about Mrs Perkins?'

Mouth downturned, she shook her head. 'No, just a day off, they say. Commander Thomas is the same as usual. Tried to pinch my bum an hour ago. He can't suspect anything. What about Ingrid?'

'I saw her briefly this morning, but then she went out. Something about hunting for some new stockings.'

Mavis raised an eyebrow. 'She'll be gone a good long while then. Like gold dust, they are.'

I had the day off so I went for a walk, just to stop myself watching the clock which seemed to have slowed as if someone had put glue on the hands. It was a dull day, overcast and threaten-ing, people walked briskly, head down. The clouds hung low, and there was a sudden shower so heavy I ducked into a shop doorway to escape being drenched. As I stood there waiting for the rain to stop, Ingrid walked past me, dry under an umbrella. She spotted me and my heart felt as if it would stop.

'Hello, Lily,' she said, stepping into the doorway. 'Can't stop, just got some new stockings. Took me ages to find them. Did you hear about Mrs Perkins?'

'I heard she's taken the day off,' I said, trying to keep my voice steady.

She shook her umbrella and closed it, coming to stand next to me. 'When I went out earlier, I was just crossing the road when I saw her fall over. It was pretty obvious she'd broken her leg and she was in a lot of pain, so I went to the hospital with her.'

So she couldn't possibly have done anything about Ingrid and Commander Thomas. My shoulders slumped.

'Gosh, are they keeping her in?' I asked.

She took a deep breath and gave a little shake of her head. 'I don't know but she was going to have a general anaesthetic to set her leg properly, so I expect so. She insisted that I not wait with her, so I left her to get my shopping.'

I thought quickly. 'What hospital is she in?'

'St Vincent's. It's not far. You going to see her?'

'Yes, I'll get some flowers or something and go to see how she's doing.'

Ingrid picked up her umbrella again, and opened it. 'Give her my love. Mustn't stop though, got more errands to do.' She ducked back into the stream of people.

Unfamiliar hospitals are always confusing and St Vincent's was no exception. After queuing at the reception desk to find out what ward Mrs Perkins was on, I got lost three times trying to find the right one. Gowned doctors and nurses scurried past me, and I was too scared to ask them where to go.

I got to the ward just in time. It took me a few minutes to find Mrs Perkins amongst the identical, precision-made beds lined up along both long walls.

She lay, pale and pained, but managed a wan smile as I approached her. She tried to sit up, but it was too much for her and she fell back against the pillows with a groan.

'Five minutes and we'll be coming for you,' a nurse said as she walked by, her starched skirt rustling like fresh newspaper.

'How are you?' I started to ask, but Mrs Perkins brushed my enquiry aside.

'No time for that, they'll be operating on my leg in a minute,' she said, her voice a shadow of its normal volume and certainty. 'You'll have to act on my behalf and go to headquarters. I've written the address on that piece of paper there.' She waved her hand at the bedside table and I tucked the address in my bag, suddenly feeling very unsure of myself.

'Will they listen to me?'

'There's a code word. Come nearer.' She beckoned me with her hand.

I bent forward so she could whisper in my ear. 'The code word is Black Buttons. Ask to see Major Villani and tell him everything you told me. He'll be able to see me tomorrow when I'm properly round from the anaesthetic, but we need to get action started now. Can you do that?'

I had no time to do more than nod when we were interrupted by the heavy footsteps of a porter approaching her bed, 'Ready, *ma cherie*?' he asked Mrs Perkins with a cheeky grin. 'It's your turn.'

Mrs Perkins nodded to him then, before she was moved, grabbed my hand and squeezed it tight. 'Can I count on you, Lily?'

I squeezed her hand back. 'Yes, Mrs Perkins, you can, and I'll come to see you tomorrow and tell you all about it.'

She closed her eyes. 'Now, go!' she commanded.

10

INGRID

The Headquarters office was in an unassuming building in a part of Paris I'd never been to before. Number 262 was a scruffy doorway between two shops, a baker's and a fishmonger's. There was no notice on the door to say what it was. I double-checked the address on the paper Mrs Perkins had given me but it seemed right.

I stood for a minute trying to pluck up courage to knock. The door had been painted grey many years before, but the paint was faded and flaking. The door knocker, one of those brass ones like a hand, hadn't been cleaned for a decade. Taking a deep breath, I straightened my clothes, quickly combed my hair then knocked loudly and waited.

A girl about my age answered the door. 'I'd like to speak to Colonel Villani, please,' I said, my voice quivering.

* * *

On the way back, I headed for my favourite café, too restless to face going to the office. I looked around at the people I passed. Was it my imagination that people seemed more tense than usual? I heard someone leave one of the cafés I passed. He called to the waiter, 'I'm leaving this city, who knows if we'll meet again.' The two shook hands and hugged, shared a '*bon chance*' then went on their way.

I had a strong coffee to give me energy. Then I had a brandy to calm down again. What must it be like, I wondered, if you were a collaborator? Although the Nazis were still a little way north of Paris, we heard more every day about the awful things they were doing and how some people were beginning to find ways to sabotage them. But we heard too that plenty of people agreed with what they were doing. It was horrible to think about.

I was deep in thought when the radio in the café was turned up for the news. All the other customers stopped speaking and we turned towards it like sheep corralled by a sheepdog. The silence as we listened was jarring after the noise of chatter and the clatter of cups.

A priest who was passing the door stopped and stepped inside to listen. He ordered a coffee using gestures only, and the barman indicated to wait until the news finished.

The newsreader spoke with slow reassuring tones. 'The situation,' he said, his French slow and easy for me to understand 'is serious, but not alarming. The enemy continues to make fierce attacks on our homeland but our troops are giving valiant resistance.' The rest of the news continued along the same lines, full of calm words that failed to do their job.

When it finished, the people in the bar began to analyse what was said.

'That sounds like empty words to me,' said one man, 'I think it's time to leave Paris.'

'Don't be too hasty,' said another. 'They will defend Paris to the last man. We will be safe. If you leave now, you might lose everything you leave behind.'

On and on it went, backwards and forwards, each person having a different take on what was happening. But of course none of us knew the true situation.

The priest finished his coffee, stood and said, 'God bless us all.' He made the sign of the cross and left, shoulders hunched.

'Sounds like a lively debate. May I buy you another brandy, Lily?' I was so deep in thought, the voice nearly made me jump out of my skin. I turned, and there was George, the nice officer who had taken time to speak to me at the initial get-together when I first arrived. I noticed again how attractive he was; broad shoulders, shiny brown hair, even white teeth and a smile you could fall into. I had to stop myself blushing just at the thoughts that went through my head.

I took a few seconds to get my emotions under control. 'No thanks, one brandy in the middle of the afternoon is more than I usually have.'

He briefly touched my arm. 'Another coffee then? And a patisserie? Cake always helps gloomy situations, I find.' He went to get them without waiting for an answer, his heels somehow sounding authoritative as he walked the few steps to the bar. I saw him choosing a cake. How some cafés managed to produce them when there were shortages everywhere was beyond me.

'Are you okay, Lily?' he asked when he sat down again, pushing the cake towards me. 'You're a bit pale.'

I so wanted to confide in him, not just about my fears about the war. I needed to just talk about my fear over Ingrid, but something stopped me. Suppose we were wrong – we'd have ruined her good name for nothing. I shook my head. 'I'm fine, just didn't sleep very well last night, that's all.'

I took a tiny bite of the cake. It was heavenly; a burst of sugar and almonds thrilled my taste buds and I just closed my eyes and gave myself over the pleasure of the moment. I put the rest down, determined to make it last when what I really wanted to do was eat it all in one mouthful.

I turned to George. 'Is there any news about whether the Germans will invade Paris? It sounded really worrying on the radio, despite all their talk of valiant soldiers and success.'

He took a sip from his tiny cup of coffee and avoided my eye. 'Nothing definite,' he said, speaking into the cup. 'I did hear though, that they are moving all the treasures from the museums.'

'I thought they'd already done that. They went to Brittany somewhere, didn't they?'

'Yes, a while ago, but it turns out that the place they used was damp, so some of the paintings are being damaged. They've got to find somewhere else.'

My hands trembled as I took the last bite of my cake, not really tasting it.

'They will get us out before the Nazis get here, won't they?' My voice was a little louder than I intended and two people at the next table stopped their conversation and turned and looked at me.

George put his hand back on my arm. 'Don't worry, it's all in hand. I can't say any more than that, I'm sure you understand.'

* * *

'They questioned me for thirty minutes Bronwyn, went over and over the details again.'

'Poor you,' she said, handing me a cup of tea, 'but they believed you?'

I put half a spoon of sugar in the tea and stirred it. 'Got a biscuit? He didn't say. Just said to leave it with him.'

'Was he nice, the bloke who questioned you?' she asked, handing over the biscuit tin, but helping herself to one first.

I put down the cup and saucer. I was fidgety after the events of the afternoon. Not just the third degree about Ingrid but guilty feelings about George. I shouldn't find him attractive when I was in love with Edward, my fiancé, the man I intended to spend the rest of my life with, should I?

So instead of sitting with my tea, I stood and fidgeted with everything in sight, I put old magazines into a neat pile even though they didn't need it; un-tangled some wires; washed and dried a glass smeared with red lipstick. 'Well, he didn't smile, that's for sure. And he took loads of notes. It made me get a little bit of an idea what it must be like to be interrogated. Without the torture, of course.'

We were alone in the kitchen at work and had checked that Ingrid was out before I updated Bronwyn on my visit to Headquarters. Although my grilling had been polite, I felt shaken thinking about it again.

'I really was under pressure to make sure what I was saying was absolutely accurate,' I said, 'I hated the thought of getting Ingrid or Major Thomas in trouble because I'd made a mistake.' I sat down again and picked up my cup.

Bronwyn and I sat quietly for a minute drinking our tea, then she put her cup and saucer down, rattling the teaspoon. 'Come on, let's go out. It's a bit changeable out there, but we can take umbrellas. We'll only sit here and worry otherwise about what might happen next.'

The weather was mild but breezy, whipping up bits of paper and other debris into tiny whirlpools. We walked through quiet backstreets, away from the hustle and bustle of central Paris. There were still people in the streets, but they were mostly older people walking slowly with their shopping bags, baguettes under their arms, or mums pushing prams, chatting to their friends or just rubbing their eyes from lack of sleep. The smell of garlic drifted out of several houses and trailed after us like a weary ghost.

'What do you think made her do it?' Bronwyn asked.

I stopped and rubbed my eye, dislodging a tiny spec of grit. 'Ingrid? Who knows? Have you got any ideas?'

Bronwyn inspected my eye, lifting my lid and peering all round. 'You're all right, it's gone. Blink a few times and you'll be in the pink.'

We were just about to cross the road when we heard someone shout, 'Hey, out of the way! Look where you're going!' A fat man on a bike that had seen better days, swerved to avoid us, narrowly missing someone who was crossing the road.

'Idiots! Fools!' he shouted over his shoulder as he cycled past us.

'That man should get himself a bell,' Bronwyn muttered.

'Do you think Ingrid wanted to do it?' I asked, as we resumed our stroll.

Bronwyn's brow furrowed. 'I don't understand. It's like this, why would she do it if she didn't want to?'

I sighed. 'I don't know, I suppose I don't want to believe she's a traitor. I wonder if she is being blackmailed.'

Bronwyn stopped in her tracks and held my arm. 'Black-mailed? Who would do that? Why?'

I took her hand away. 'I don't know. I don't know anything, but what if someone's got something on her?'

'What, like an illegitimate child or something?'

'Or she might be protecting family, if they're Jewish. I told you about the name I found in that book she carries around. What if it's her real name? Or if she got it from a member of her family who is a German Jew? It's not impossible.'

Bronwyn got out a cigarette and lit it, cupping her hand to stop the wind blowing the match out. She took a big drag and blew out the smoke as if it were the most luxurious thing possible. 'So, someone would be blackmailing her to give them information or they'd kill her family. Is that what you're thinking?'

I moved to the other side of her to be away from the cigarette smoke, which always made me cough. 'It might be. But one thing's for sure, we'll never know. I can't see them telling us. Mind you, Mavis keeps her ear to the ground so she'll tell us if she hears anything.'

I was silent for a while as we walked, my thoughts returning to George. I kept thinking about his broad shoulders, the way he really seemed to listen to what I was saying as if it were important, and the way his eyes softened when he looked at me.

Bronwyn noticed, of course, nothing gets past her. 'What've you been up to, *cariad*? You've got a glint in your eye that I recognise.'

'Nothing, I was just thinking about Edward,' I lied, and hoped that it wouldn't be an unlucky thing to do. Edward, I reminded myself, was the man I loved, the best, kindest man in the world.

* * *

Bronwyn and I had just got back to base and taken off our coats when we heard two cars draw up outside. It had just started to rain and the windows were spotted, frustrating my attempts to see what was happening outside clearly. The driver of one car was opening the rear door of his car and a man in an official uniform stepped out and looked up at the building as if it would answer some crucial question for him. The doors of the other car opened and four police officers got out.

'Military police!' whispered Bronwyn, who was peering over my shoulder. 'I wonder if they're coming for Ingrid.'

All five men marched into our building and we heard their

heavy footsteps getting closer as they mounted the stairs. Our tension rose with every step.

They went immediately into Major Thomas's office.

'Where's Ingrid?' Bronwyn asked, her voice still hushed although we were alone in the kitchen.

I tried to picture the duty rota. 'I think she's on duty, so she'll be in the telephone room. Do you think we should warn her?'

Bronwyn frowned and put her hands on her hips. 'Warn her? Are you crazy? She might be a traitor, costing the lives of our soldiers. I'm not being funny or anything, but if you try to warn her, I'll knock you out.'

I glared at her, but I knew she was right. The letter drop incident proved it, there was no other explanation. I wished and wished there was. At the very least Ingrid was likely to be subject to hours of questioning, at worst she might be hung for a traitor.

Without a word between us, Bronwyn grabbed my arm and pulled me into a nearby door. It was the storage cupboard, next to the landing and stairs. All manner of things were stacked on shelves: bedding; stationery; two typewriters; odds and ends of crockery and cutlery; and sealed boxes with no identification on them.

'Keep the light off!' Bronwyn hissed. 'Ee can see through the keyhole and we don't want anyone spotting the light.'

She'd have made a good spy herself.

Several times people walked by and we held our breath, expecting to be caught at any moment. Once someone tried to get in the cupboard, but we held the handle tight and after what seemed like hours of tugging, we heard them go off muttering oaths. We took it in turns to spy through the keyhole. Bending down soon gave us backaches as if we were a couple of eighty-year-olds.

To make our espionage even harder, the sound of the rain

increased, making it difficult to hear what was going on out of sight.

But then we heard a door open and footsteps going across a floor above us. Like idiots we looked up as if the ceiling were suddenly transparent.

'Is that Major Thomson's door?' Bronwyn asked. 'I think it was.'

There were loud voices and we heard Major Thomson saying, 'This is outrageous! Let me go!'

More noises like furniture being pushed aside and more protests, then we saw Major Thomson being taken down the stairs, a Redcap holding each arm. His back was rigid and he marched between them as if he were on a parade ground.

'He's in handcuffs!' Bronwyn whispered. 'If they've arrested him, it'll be Ingrid next.'

We lost sight of them, but within two or three minutes the officer came back upstairs and joined up with the other two Redcaps.

They strode into the telephonists' room. The door closed behind them with a slam.

We heard voices, some loud, others soft, but weren't able to make out what they were saying. Then we heard a loud bang, and the sound of a chair tipping over onto the floor. Then the sound of a woman sobbing.

It seemed like ages afterwards, but was probably only a couple of minutes when the door to the telephonists' room opened again and Ingrid walked out.

'She's got handcuffs as well!' I whispered. 'And there's a Redcap either side of her!'

Bronwyn nudged me out of the way and bent down to see. 'That officer's following them. Come on!'

She grabbed my arm again and pulled me out of the cupboard. Tiptoeing, we followed the four of them down the stairs, although the men's boots made so much noise it's doubtful they'd have heard us anyway.

Ingrid stopped every few steps. Still sobbing, she wiped her eyes as best she could with her hands fixed together.

'What's going on?' I shouted. 'Where are you taking Ingrid?'

All four of them stopped as if a tightrope barred their paths. They turned back and I wanted to vanish, my mouth dry as cotton, but it was too late. The Redcaps stood stock-still, but Ingrid looked at us pleadingly, biting her bottom lip so hard a tiny drop of blood appeared. It was the senior officer who spoke, eyes cold as a tomb.

'None of your business, young ladies. Get back to your flat.'

'But we were just...' Bronwyn started. If I didn't know her so well, I'd have thought she was completely confident, but a slight shake in her hand, which still gripped mine, gave away her emotion.

The officer waved his hand dismissively. 'Never mind what you were going to do, go back to your rooms!'

All four of them turned and started walking down the stairs again. I made to go back but Bronwyn was having none of it. 'Come on, we're going to see what happens,' she said, squeezing my hand so tight I almost cried out in pain.

Hardly daring to breathe, we followed them right to the front door where they paused. There was no sign of Major Thomas and his Redcaps. Presumably, they'd already gone in the first car.

'Where's the second car?' The officer growled, impatiently, arrogantly. It was a busy time of day and the traffic was heavier than usual, with barely a gap to be seen in either direction. Buses, cars, horse and carts, and bicycles all jostled to get through. The noise was deafening. The air smelled of petrol, rain and horse droppings.

Ingrid tugged and pulled at the soldiers who were holding her by the arms. They held her so tight she squealed with pain.

'Don't be so rough!' I shouted, making them jump.

In that moment they lost concentration. Ingrid yanked her arms free.

She ran to the kerb and quickly looked around as the soldiers reached for her.

A bus was heading towards where she stood. Without hesitation she stepped in front of it.

11

ESCAPE

The door burst open and a tall, handsome man strode in. He was wearing a thin grey sweater and dark grey trousers. His eyes were grey-green and his dirty blond hair threatened to fall over them.

'Your transport out of here awaits, ladies,' he said, his tone urgent. 'Don't be fooled by my mufti, I'm RAF and I'll be your driver to the muster point just outside Paris.'

Mrs Perkins came into the room. 'Squadron Leader Robson? Delighted to meet you.' She shook his hand vigorously.

'Lovely to meet you. Call me Jim.' He made a sweeping gesture with his hands indicating the door. 'Right, girls, disconnect everything, grab your bags. We're leaving immediately.'

Although we'd been waiting for the order and worrying that the German army would arrive before we left, there was still a flurry of panic as we rushed around picking up things. I was grateful for the order we'd received when we first arrived to give anything we'd written to Mrs Perkins. There was nothing for us to destroy, although the people in the office upstairs certainly had plenty.

The airman stopped us. 'One bag each girls, we can't take any more, and make it snappy. I've just heard that the Germans are approaching Paris. They are meeting no resistance. We've got to get out of here fast!'

This made us panic even more. I cursed myself for not thinking of this and realised that all my most precious things were divided between my kitbag and a carpet bag I'd got for a song in a market.

'Chop! Chop!' the airman shouted. 'We're leaving right now.' He came and physically pushed the slowest girls towards the door. I gave the room a final glance. I thought sadly that I would never again work anywhere so beautiful with such a wonderful city just outside the door.

I'd miss the few friends I'd made in the city; the barman at Chez Nous; the elderly Jewish couple with all their stories; the people at the soup kitchen.

I was also still reeling from Ingrid's suicide and the part I had played in it. Seeing her battered and bloody body under the wheels of the bus was a scene that played again and again in my head, keeping me awake at night. Bronwyn constantly told me I'd done the right thing reporting her; she was a spy, a traitor, putting our people at risk. I knew she was right but Ingrid always seemed vulnerable somehow, and I believed being a spy was not what she wanted to do. But her death meant that we'd probably never know the truth.

'Hurry up!' Jim shouted again, running his hands through his hair, a deep frown between his eyebrows. His eyes darted again and again to the window as if expecting the army to be marching towards us any minute.

Our footsteps echoed eerily as we hurried down the stairs. We were scared of each noise, glancing over our shoulder every few steps. The building already had an abandoned feel. Some doors were open and the rooms seemed deserted with only basic furniture to be seen; the buzz of life extinguished.

People had been leaving the city for five days. First went the expensive cars driven by chauffeurs with ladies holding their jewellery boxes sitting in splendour on the otherwise empty back seat. Children stood and gazed at them enviously, imagining themselves riding in such luxury.

'Look at them nobs,' Mavis said, 'got their jewellery but I can't see any food or water. They mad or what?'

I nodded. 'I heard a rumour that they're so used to getting what they want any time, they expect to be able to buy food and drink on the way. Probably expect high-class restaurant service, too.'

Mavis snorted. 'They'll be lucky. From what we've 'eard there's precious little to spare. Still, I expect someone'll rip 'em off and good luck to 'em. Idiots.'

The next day more cars had passed by, but these ones didn't seem quite so expensive. They were a bit more laden, with whole families seated comfortably. 'Not as rich as yesterday's lot, are they?' Mavis said. 'Weird, isn't it? As if some'ow the orders were to let the rich go first.'

'Well, there are plenty of notices telling people how to leave the city,' I said.

'Yeah,' she replied, 'but they're not about cars, are they? They're stupid, telling people which station to leave from when they 'ave no idea 'ow to get to the right station with all their luggage. I'd be like them, wanting to leave from the nearest one.'

'But the radio gives people regular updates.'

She looked at me like I was stupid. 'Who's thinking straight at the moment? Like us, they must 'ear 'orror stories from refugees from further north who are passing through. It's a bloody mess, that's what it is.'

The third day it was the old cars spluttering and jerking their way down the road, laden with people and all their household goods. They often had suitcases, bags and even mattresses tied to the roof. They wove their laden way at snail's pace through the increasing number of people on foot.

The fourth and fifth days were people using every imaginable means of transport – bicycles, motorbikes, prams, trolleys. We even saw a man pushing a lawn mower, his worldly goods precariously strapped up the handle. Although we'd seen a trickle of country people each day, the fourth and fifth days were when the bulk of people from the countryside passed through the city with their farm carts and horses. The carts were piled high with all their belongings, and mattresses bounced up and down on top, sometimes with a child enjoying being king of the castle. We saw very elderly people being pushed in prams; sleeping children being carried in their parents' arms, heads flopping sideways; and people on crutches struggling to keep up with their families. It was hard to keep the tears from flowing as we watched.

There, in the midst of the fifth day chaos, was the lorry we were to travel in.

'Sorry it's not a luxury limo,' Jim said. 'It'll be uncomfortable and I'm not at all sure it's very roadworthy but it's the best we've got. Hop in.'

We threw our kitbags in and jumped into the lorry. It reminded me of our arrival at basic training. We'd been dressed in our best, high heel shoes and all, and none of us fit enough to jump into a lorry. What a difference that training had made.

The lorry had a metal frame with canvas covering the top, and a canvas flap at the back. Wooden benches on the side were all there was in the way of seating. It certainly wasn't comfortable, but I felt guilty about having transport at all when so many people were on foot. The weather had been unusually warm for the last few days and people were sweating as they struggled under their burdens.

Jim closed the canvas flap when we got in. 'No point in making yourselves targets, girls. A lot of people would try to get in if they knew there was free space.'

'Would that be terrible?' I asked when he was walking round to the cab. 'Some of these people are desperate.'

'It's like this, see,' said Bronwyn, 'you let one in, they all want to come in and before you know it we're thrown out and the lorry is stolen. Better to keep a low profile.'

The lorry started with a bang from the exhaust, and we jumped nervously.

'How far is Dunkirk anyway?' one of the other girls asked.

'I think it's about three hundred miles,' I said.

Her eyes widened. 'Three hundred miles! We're going so slow what with all these refugees that it'll take us a week to get there.'

She had a point.

'I heard that there have been so many evacuees from Holland and Belgium they have slowed the Allied troops down. They've been told to go back home,' Amanda said, reaching into her bag and producing some boiled sweets. 'Would anyone like one of these?'

''Ave many of the refugees gone 'ome then?' Mavis asked.

'I don't think so, not the last I heard anyway. People that far north have had a lot of bombing and they're too scared to go back. So would I be.'

We all lapsed into silence, worried that the bombing would catch up with us. I looked around and everyone sat with slumped shoulders and frowns on their faces.

'Come on,' I said, 'no point in worrying. Let's think of something else. What's the first thing you're going to do when you get home?'

'Find some fish and chips.' Mavis said.

'Go and see Mummy and Daddy,' Amanda said.

Bronwyn thought for a minute. 'Dunno. Might go back to

Swansea, though I'm not keen. I suppose it depends where they send us next. Plenty of places I haven't been. That's if everywhere's not already bombed to bits. What about you, Lily?'

'I'd love it if Edward had some leave at the same time, but that's probably pie in the sky even if he's escaped from the prisoner-of-war camp. I really want to see Mum again.' I fanned my face. 'It's getting really hot in here. Do you think we can get away with opening the flap a bit?'

Bronwyn opened it just a couple of inches and the breeze was a real tonic. We took it in turns to sit near the gap, look out the back, and cool ourselves. The line of people escaping Paris seemed endless. I heard not just French spoken, but Dutch and Flemish too.

'Some of these people must have been walking for days,' I said, 'they're exhausted.'

Amanda nodded. 'And in this heat, they must be so dry and so tired.' She looked around. 'Talking of which, I think Jim said something about a jerrycan of water. It must be under that seat at the back.'

As she spoke there was a loud banging and shouting. I peeked out of the back of the lorry. It was people wanting us to take them in the lorry.

'Keep calm, girls,' Jim shouted from the front, 'just ignore them.'

We kept as still and quiet as possible and eventually they gave up hope. It was hard to know what was worse, them trying or them giving up.

Progress to the muster point was very slow with banging on the lorry happening again from time to time. Heat and desperation made people reckless. With each passing minute we seemed to withdraw more into ourselves and not a word was spoken, even when the water was passed round.

'Do you think they've left it too late for us to get back to Blighty?' Mavis asked. 'What'll 'appen if the Germans catch us?'

No one answered her.

After what seemed hours, Jim shouted, 'Sit tight, girls. We're at the muster station but I can't see our group. I'll go and investigate.'

'Bloody 'ell,' Mavis said, 'what if they've gone without us? What'll we do?'

'We can walk,' someone said.

'What three 'undred miles? In this 'eat? With our kitbags? What about trains? Are they still running?'

Amanda offered her remaining boiled sweets round again. 'We might get a train to the coast, but we can't get one up as far as Dunkirk. There is no way of knowing if the German army has headed that way. We'd need to enter the area carefully. In a train we might just get steamed right into the hornets' nest.'

We lapsed into silence again, but a minute later Jim was back, sticking his head through the canvas flap. 'Change of plans, girls, I'm taking you to the Gare du Nord.'

It was difficult to get out of the lorry when we reached the station because so many people were milling about. They were checking around frantically for news of train departures. The station had stopped selling tickets and that caused confusion as people wondered if it meant that the trains wouldn't run. We heard anxious parents calling for their children who had become separated from them; incomprehensible messages from the loudspeaker, and the general roar of hundreds of worried people.

'Come with me,' Jim shouted, and we followed him, pushing our way through the crowds to a platform. By the time we got there we were bruised and battered from walking into suitcases, or falling over them and landing on the floor or, worse still, landing on someone else and knocking them over too.

Eventually, we all congregated around Jim. 'Right, on that train now!' he said. 'Good luck to you all. See you in Blighty.'

We all clambered on the train. We four stayed together, but the other girls we'd travelled in the truck with were spread in different carriages. The train was so packed it was hard to imagine anyone else could get on. Some people had their belongings tied up in sheets and we heard pots and pans rattling together as people walked by. Children grizzled and were comforted or told off by their parents.

We squeezed into a corner, apologising all the time for treading on toes and crashing into people. The air in the corridor was full of smells: sweat, garlic, pee and bad breath all mingled so strongly I tried to breathe through my mouth to avoid the urge to vomit. My clothes stuck to me even more than they had before and my swollen feet ached in my sturdy ATS shoes.

We stood for another thirty minutes, all the time getting more squashed as people crowded onto the train. Then, at last, we heard the train's whistle and we slowly started to chug away. Even then we saw people running along the platform trying to get on.

Dispirited, thirsty and tired, we stood silently, surrounded by people as tired as ourselves who were chatting or somehow sleeping standing up.

Several times we passed roads that were packed with people running from the Germans. They snaked for endless slow-moving miles seemingly with no beginning or end. Cars moved no quicker than those on foot who blocked their way. Those walking dragged their feet, heavy with luggage and children. The sun, usually so welcome, shone mercilessly upon them.

The train rattled along the track with frequent and unexplained stops which got everyone talking. I noticed Amanda listening to a conversation near her. Her face went pale and she turned to us. 'I hope to goodness I'm wrong, but these people are talking about where this train is going.' She took a deep breath. 'We're on the wrong train.'

We all looked at her in stunned disbelief.

'We'll have to get off at the next stop and find a way back.' Bronwyn said. 'I'm trying to keep calm, but I'm getting ready to scream to tell you the truth.'

'That damn Jim!' Mavis said, her voice an octave or two higher than normal. 'Why the 'ell didn't he check properly? He pushed us onto this train.'

Amanda sat down on her kitbag. 'We might as well make ourselves comfortable until the next stop. We'll get off there, though goodness knows when we can get a train in the right direction.'

We struggled to get off the train at the next station, Essonne. People were crowded everywhere, blocking the corridors with their bodies and their luggage. The whole country seemed to be on the move. We stepped over people, occasionally stepped on them, calling out apologies as we struggled to find a way to the door to get off. Then we struggled some more as people fought to get on the train at that end. The smell of smoke from the engine mingled with the smell of sweat seemed stronger as people lugged their cases and bags aboard. The noise of cases banging, doors slamming and people shouting instructions to each other added to the general sense of panic. We were definitely somewhere we didn't want to be. Weary, we stood on the platform and gave a collective sigh of relief.

'Thank goodness, fresh air!' Amanda said, fanning herself. 'Trouble is, now we have to find the right train. I'll go and see what I can find out.' She headed towards the railway building.

'Oh, blimey,' said Mavis, 'none of the others got off. They can't 'ave realised they were on the wrong train. What'll we do?'

Bronwyn and I looked at each other. 'There's nothing we can

do,' I said, 'we'll just have to hope they realise soon and get off at the next station.'

About twenty other people got off the train at the same place as us. Some were greeted by people they knew, and we saw them head off in a car or horse and cart. Others picked up their luggage and started to walk.

'They look done for already,' Mavis said. 'I wonder how long they've been travelling.'

Bronwyn nodded. 'I wonder why they're getting off here. We can't be a lot further south, though to tell the truth I've no idea where we exactly are. Perhaps they're walking to relatives they can stay with.'

'I expected a lot more traffic on the road,' I said.

'Me, too,' said Mavis. 'Maybe it's that people 'ave gone on the main ones. Who knows?'

After the noise and bustle of the departing train and other refugees, the station seemed eerily quiet. We heard a tractor some distance off, and a cricket sawed loudly somewhere nearby, but that was all.

12

THE LOST GIRL

We were checking we had all out luggage, when Bronwyn said, 'Lily, there's a little girl there on her own.'

Sure enough, a little girl in a thin cotton dress was standing half behind a pillar plastered with peeling advertisements. Her shoes were well worn, probably hand-me-downs, and she had a green ribbon in her hair held in place by a kirby grip. She was sucking her thumb and clutching a ragged toy rabbit. I guessed she was three or four years old. There were no adults left on the station apart from us.

I went over and bent down to get to her level.

'Are you lost?' I asked, in my best French. She didn't answer but just held her rabbit tighter to her body looking anywhere but at me. I tried again. 'Hello, what's your name?' Still no answer.

'Anyone got a sweet?' I asked the others. They dug around in their pockets and Bronwyn found a wrapped boiled sweet. I held it out to the girl. 'Would you like this?' I asked.

She grabbed it at lightning speed and hid it quickly in a pocket in her dress.

I smiled at her. 'What's your name, little one?'

'Elise,' she said.

Feeling stupid, I held out my hand. 'Nice to meet you, Elise. I'm Lily and these are my friends Bronwyn and Mavis.' They came over and shook her hand too, saying hello in French. At that moment Amanda came back.

'There's no one in the station and from the look of a tatty timetable on the wall, there are no more trains until tomorrow. Heaven knows if that timetable is up to date though.'

Only then did she seem to notice Elise. 'Who's this?' she asked. 'Where's she come from? Who's she with?'

I shrugged. 'Her name's Elise and we haven't learned any more yet, but there's no one else about. Seems like she's got left behind.'

'Well,' said Bronwyn, 'if there's no more trains today, her mum won't be coming back for her. We'd better try to find someone who can look after her.'

I bent down to Elise's level again. 'Elise, where do you live?'

She ignored my question, but got the boiled sweet out of her pocket and carefully unwrapped it. Keeping an eye on us as if we might steal it from her, she quickly popped it into her mouth. Her eyes closed for a minute as if in delight at the taste. Then she slowly smoothed the wrapper, folded it and put it back in her pocket. I asked her a few more questions but got no more information from her.

'We'd better go into the village,' Mavis said, 'perhaps someone will know her and in any case we need to find lodgings for the night.'

A sudden chill ran through me. 'We don't even know if we're in an occupied area. The Germans may be in the village for all we know.'

Amanda held up her hand. 'We'd know, trust me. They'd have been here at the station overseeing things, clumping around in their big boots, intimidating everyone. But that doesn't mean they won't be here soon. They were beginning to march through Paris when we left and this place isn't that many miles from there. We have no way of knowing which direction they'll head in. We need to get off to Dunkirk as quickly as possible.' She nodded towards Elise. 'We're not here to babysit.'

'Not being funny or nothing,' Bronwyn chipped in, 'but what about our uniforms? Should we get changed into civvies? We'll get captured for sure if the Germans see us dressed like this.'

I held Elise's hand. 'Good point. Let's go into the building and change.'

Twenty minutes later, we were on the outskirts of the village, dressed in our everyday clothes. Elise continued to hold my hand, but still didn't speak. I hoped she would show some signs of recognition as we walked through the village. It didn't happen.

'Let's find the *mairie*, the town hall,' said Amanda. 'If there is anyone there, they can help us.'

Light clouds covered the sun, sending biblical rays of light fanning across the sky. The village houses, many in a poor state, took on a warm, romantic appearance that belied the hard life the villagers lived. Chickens scratched around in several gardens, and we heard pigs snuffling about occasionally. Other gardens just had flowers or vegetable patches out front. As we walked, a farm cart passed by, pulled by a tired horse whose head hung low and whose pace was slow. The driver doffed his hat at us, and we got an air-kiss from a young lad who sat with his legs dangling from the rear of the cart.

A stone bridge just wide enough for a horse and cart spanned a narrow river that ran through the village. As we walked, the village church rang the half-past.

'I reckon the *mairie* will be closed by now,' Mavis said.

Amanda nodded. 'You're probably right, but we have to start somewhere and there's no one around.'

When we turned the corner we found a small group of men playing boule in a dusty square in front of the *mairie*. They were older men, with bent backs and flat caps. They wore hand-knitted jumpers under their shabby jackets. The scene was timeless and I was convinced that war or no war, this exact same scene would be here in a hundred years' time. The men were chatting and laughing and didn't hear our approach at first, but when they did they stopped in their tracks.

'*Bonjour*, Mesdamoiselles!' one said, giving us a toothless grin. 'I haven't seen you before.'

'*Bonjour*, Monsieur. Can you help us?'

We shook hands and kissed cheeks with each of the men in the time honoured way.

I indicated Elise. 'We were travelling to Dunkirk but got on the wrong train. When we got off, we found this little girl all alone. Do you recognise her?'

They all shook their heads. 'No, never seen her before and we know everyone in this village,' one old man said. 'If she was at the station, she may come from any of the villages around here. It's the only station in the area. Her mum will be hunting for her.'

I looked down at Elise who was rubbing her eyes. There was a stone wall nearby and I sat on it and pulled her on my knee. 'I need a wee,' she said so quietly I almost didn't hear her.

'She needs to visit a bathroom,' I said to the men, 'is there one she can use here? I expect we could do with one too. And we need somewhere to stay for the night. There are no more trains today so even if Elise's mother is looking for her she won't be able to get here.'

The men had a quick conversation in French, too fast for me to understand. Several times they looked at Elise, then me and the others. Then one, who said his name was Paul, turned to me. 'You can all come with me. My wife will take you in, although it'll be the floor to sleep on tonight, I'm afraid.'

We walked behind Paul, unsure of a welcome. His pace was slow, fitting his stooped back and bow legs. After a few minutes Elise started to fidget with what my mum called 'the toilet dance'. Then without warning, she squatted down at the side of the road, pulled her knickers aside and peed there and then – a steaming puddle the only evidence. It was expertly done and I felt not a little envious. It had taken just a minute and she quickly held my hand again. We followed Paul as he plodded determinedly along. He hadn't even noticed.

Mavis moved back to walk beside me. ''Ow do we know 'im or 'is missus aren't German spies?' she asked, her voice low enough so Paul couldn't overhear.

Our experience with Ingrid meant that spies were never far from our mind. On the train we'd been jumpy and paranoid, constantly checking around as if spies had a big sign on their foreheads. Stupid.

'Well, they might be,' I said, 'but we'll leave tomorrow morning early to see if Elise's mum is on the first train. There are no phones here, not even electricity. So if they're spies, they'll be lucky to get a message through before we head off. I think we can risk it.'

Paul led us to one of the small cottages we had passed earlier. Roses were beginning to bloom around the doorway and cottage flowers surrounded the building like a skirt. The remainder of both gardens were given over to well-tended vegetable plots. A wooden shed, leaning to one side, stood in one corner and the lavvy was in another. A tin bath hung from one side of the lav.

Paul's wife, Reini, peered at us warily as we stood on her doorstep. Spare flesh hung around her elbows and her well-worn wedding ring slid around her finger as she moved. She wiped her hands on her flowery apron as Paul explained the situation, then stood aside to let us in.

'Come in, come in,' she said with a smile, 'and a little one!' She smiled at Elise. 'Lost your mummy, have you? We'll help you find her.' Elise's response was to hold my hand even tighter and hide behind my legs.

The kitchen reminded me a lot of our old one, before we moved to the new corporation estate that was still my home. It had a wood-burning stove for cooking and heating, a deep sink, and a tall cupboard for plates and saucepans. An oilcloth-covered table and chairs stood in the middle of the room. Cotton curtains, so well washed you could almost see through them, waved gently at the open window. A small settee was pushed against one wall.

Reini got out glasses and poured us all some water from a jug. I noticed there was no tap, so guessed she got water from a pump in the garden.

When we were seated, she leaned back against the sink, her hands on her bony hips, her dress hanging loosely from her frame. 'So,' she said, 'it's obvious you're not French. Where are you from? American? German?'

We almost jumped up and that last question. We wondered how much we should give away.

'Come on,' she said, 'cat got your tongue?'

I took a deep breath. 'We are in the ATS, the British army. Our uniforms are in our bags here. We are trying to get to Dunkirk so we can get back home before we are caught by the Germans. We got on the wrong train by mistake. Then we found Elise who had somehow been left behind at the station.'

She paused for a minute as if trying to weigh up the truth of my words. 'Let me see your uniform,' she said.

I opened my bag and took it out. Creased and a bit grubby, it wasn't a great testament to the ATS. She glanced at it, then nodded and without another word she turned and got out plates and cutlery. She gave us some cheese and baguette along with an apple. 'It's not much, but it's all I can spare,' she said. 'You can sleep here tonight, then you'll need to be on your way. Who knows when the Bosch will arrive. I can't risk you being here if they appear.'

We quickly realised that the kitchen also served as the only living room. As night fell, Reini spread blankets on the lino floor and gave us more to cover ourselves. Then with a last '*Bonne nuit*' she slowly climbed the stairs to her bed, followed by Paul who had had little to say for himself all evening.

'Come on, Elise,' I said, trying to get her to sleep on the settee, but she protested and refused to let go of my hand. I cuddled her and quietly told her the Cinderella story until she slept in my arms. I loved the feel of her small wiry body and the smell of her hair. It made me think of Edward all over again. If we both lived through this war, I hoped we would be married and have a family soon. It was ages since I'd heard from him, and I had no idea if he was even alive still. I wondered if family were notified if prisoners-of-war died.

I sensed my thoughts dragging my mood down and shook myself. Self-pity gets you nowhere as my mum always said.

I gently put Elise to sleep on the settee and lay down on a blanket on the floor. It might have been hard, but I was asleep in seconds. My dreams were a muddle of trains; running from tanks; Edward wounded and in pain; and hordes of German soldiers. I tossed and turned and woke feeling like I hadn't slept at all.

Over breakfast of baguette and jam, we discussed with Reini how to find Elise's home.

'She must be from one of the villages round here,' she said. 'You need to visit them. There are four within walking distance but it'll take you all day by the time you get there and check. Probably more if you have to knock on a lot of doors.'

Amanda's eyes opened wide. 'But we can't do that, we have to get to Dunkirk quickly. We have to get back home.'

Reini bit her lip. 'In that case, the best thing you can do is go to the Convent of the Blessed Lady in St Auxious just west of here. They take in unwanted children.'

Elise was listening to this conversation and started to cry, clutching my hand again.

'Elise,' I said, 'what is your other name?' She just cried more and said nothing. 'Where do you live, *ma chou*?'

She shook her head.

I looked at Reini. 'If we take her to the convent, her mother won't know where she is.'

Bronwyn spoke up. 'We'll put a notice up in the station, that's where she'll come first.'

Reini nodded. 'And ask the postman to enquire in all the villages he delivers to. He might know something and he can spread the word of where she is.'

The day promised to be hot as we set off down the country road, but at that early hour the air was pleasantly silky and welcoming. We walked along a small road flanked by fields of wheat and vegetables. I'd never lived in the countryside and couldn't identify all the crops growing. The trees gently waved us on our way and birds sang to us.

'It's a lovely day,' I said, swinging Elise round.

Her giggle was a wonderful sound.

'Lovely or not, we have to get moving, and fast,' Amanda said, picking up the pace. 'If she can't keep up, we'll take it in turns to carry her.'

It didn't take long to walk back to the station. Of course, the train was an hour late and we amused Elise by playing any games we knew and singing songs. Amanda had a wide knowledge of both.

As we waited, more and more people appeared at the station, some weighed down with luggage, others obviously waiting to meet people. Talk all around us was of the war, evacuation and the German army. We regularly checked to see if anyone recognised Elise, but with no luck.

Then the train finally arrived. After the hustle and bustle of people getting on and off, we were left with no one searching for our little lost girl.

'Bloody hell,' Bronwyn said, 'we'll have to find someone to take her. We can't put a notice up until we know where we'll leave her.'

Elise had been expecting to see her mother and sobbed when she didn't appear – heartbroken and inconsolable. There was nothing for it but to set out again searching for a saviour for her. And us. We spoke to the last person to get off the train, asking for help.

'There's a convent that way,' he said, pointing down a country lane, 'they take in kids, so I've heard.' A mile further on we saw a sign to the convent, although turning down the lane we couldn't see it at all. Amanda kept looking at her watch and sighing and Bronwyn and Mavis were just as tense. I was responsible for insisting we find somewhere for Elise.

'I'm sorry,' I said, speaking in English so Elise wouldn't understand me, 'let's just give it a few hours to find somewhere for her? Maybe the convent will take her anyway.'

Mavis gave me a shadow of a smile. 'I feel like you, wanting to make sure she's okay. But she's one child and there are four of us. We're putting ourselves in danger being 'ere. I say we give it four hours then we leave 'er with the nearest reasonable adult. Okay?'

I nodded, my heart heavy, but just then help appeared. We heard the rattle of an engine and a butcher's van pulled up behind us. A man in a grey cotton jacket and white hat wound down the window and put his head out.

'You girls going to the next village?' he asked, his French accent so strong I struggled to understand him. 'I'm going there. Want a lift?'

'We're going to the convent,' I said. 'Can you drop us off there?'

'Hop in the back.' He got out of the van to open the rear doors. 'I've done most of my deliveries so there's room if a couple of you come in the front with me. Maybe you with the little one, it'll be a bit tight otherwise.'

The others squeezed in the back of the van amongst the metal trays and the bags of meat waiting to be delivered. Even without going in there, I smelled the blood and offal. I counted myself lucky to be going in the front.

'Why are you going to the convent?' asked the driver, who said his name was Pierre.

'We are on our way to Dunkirk but we found Elise here at the station and we're trying to find her mother. Do you recognise her?'

He turned and looked at her properly, taking his eyes off the road for a moment too long. The steering wheel veered to the right and before we knew it, we were on the verge, the engine stalled.

He turned the key and the engine started again, but the wheels refused to turn. He sighed heavily. 'The earth here is like the Somme, one shower of rain and it turns into mud. We'll have to do a push start.'

I thought about the time ticking by, and our arrival at Dunkirk being delayed even more. The trouble was, we were never told what to expect there. For all we knew the Germans might already be occupying the whole area.

As we got out and opened the rear doors for the others to help, I asked, 'Monsieur Pierre, have you heard news of the German advance in the last few days?'

He stopped in his tracks, his hand still on the rear door handle. His voice lowered. 'They've taken Paris, it's completely occupied.

What, I ask myself, is the French army doing? Drinking cognac while they sit on their backsides?'

We shrugged and he opened the door. 'Come on, girls,' I said, 'we're stuck. We have to push the van off the verge.'

They unwound their limbs and groaned as they got out, stretching their legs and backs.

We heaved and pushed, and a few minutes later, we were on our way again. Another ten minutes of bone shaking and we arrived at the convent walls.

We hugged Pierre and thanked him for his kindness, then faced the heavy double doors ahead of us. They were some sort of pale wood, centuries old with scratches and scrapes to show their history. It was easy to imagine horses and carts being driven through, their careless driver grazing the sides in his hurry.

I took a deep breath, knowing what I was going to say would cause dissent. 'Pierre says Paris has fallen to the Germans.'

The others looked at me in disbelief and no one spoke for a few seconds.

'It's no surprise,' Bronwyn finally said, 'but it's still a shock. Do you think we're doing the right thing going to Dunkirk? It's a lot further north than Paris. It might be occupied as well by now.'

Although she didn't understand English, Elise had picked up the tension and tears started to slowly run down her cheeks. She wiped them away with the ears of her cloth rabbit and looked at me with big pleading eyes.

I nodded towards her, and put a finger to my lips. 'Let's talk about this later. For now, we'll see if the convent can help.' I switched to French. 'Don't worry, Elise, we'll make sure you're safe. Do you know this place?'

She shook her head.

'I don't know about you,' said Mavis, hitching her rucksack higher on her back, 'but I'd be proper afraid if I was her. Lost her mum, dragged around the country by four girls she doesn't know and not as much as a spare pair of knickers to her name.'

'Come on, let's get on with it!' Amanda said, a sharpness in her voice I'd never heard before. She knocked loudly at the door.

No response.

She knocked again. We waited. Nothing.

A third time. Still no response.

We rattled the door handles but they were locked shut.

Amanda slammed her hand palm hard against the door and cursed. 'Come on, we'll have to see if there's another way in.'

We started to walk around the six foot high wall surrounding the rest of the building. Where there were windows, they were high, so impossible to see into. But most of the wall had none so we guessed it enclosed a garden.

'If there's a chapel in 'ere, it must for their use only. The locals would never find a way in,' Mavis said. 'I don't get a sense they're welcoming to local people.'

We looked at each other glumly.

All five us all walked around the outside of the convent, hoping for another way in. In one wall there was a sort of hatch where you could pull down a basket-like flap and then close it again.

'What the 'ell's that?' Mavis asked, opening and closing the flap. 'Do they get their food delivered that way?'

Amanda touched Mavis's arm. 'I know what it is, I've seen them before. When local girls have a baby they can't keep, they put them in there, close the hatch and then the nuns collect them.'

Tears came to Mavis's eyes and I remembered it wasn't so long back that she'd had an abortion. I put my arm around her. 'It's hard to hear these things, isn't it? Let's hope the nuns are kind to them and give them a good education. And I expect some get adopted too. At least the girls are less likely to get rejected this way.'

Mavis bit back a sob. 'Poor babies,' she said, 'poor mothers.' Her back sagged and she wiped her eyes. Elise let go of my hand, and held on to Mavis's hand instead. She handed Mavis her rabbit.

Mavis held it and kissed Elise's hand. 'Oh, little one,' she said in French, 'you are looking after me. What a kind girl you are.' She picked Elise up and held her tight as we started to walk again.

We should have gone the other way because we were almost back where we started when we saw a small garden gate, half hidden by ivy. The latch opened first time.

We crept inside, heads low, checking this way and that like a bunch of amateur criminals. Ahead of us were three paths. One led to what was clearly the main building, another to a garden shed and greenhouse and a third to we couldn't see where. There were no flowers in sight although we saw several vegetable beds and a big chicken run surrounded by barbed wire.

Amanda straightened her back, and set her jaw firmly. 'Come on, we're not breaking any laws. Let's go and find someone.'

As we neared the building we heard chanting, at first a low hum then it grew louder. It was a beautiful sound, hypnotic, soothing.

'We must be near the chapel,' Bronwyn said, her voice a whisper. 'They won't appreciate being interrupted.'

Amanda just shrugged her shoulders and we carried on round until we found the chapel. It had a beautiful oak door, elaborately carved with angels and devils. The polished brass handles were like miniature hands holding poles, which we turned slowly. The hinges squealed so loudly they drowned out the chanting and the door dragged on the floor where it had already scraped a hollow arc. We held back, expecting some sort of response, but the chanting continued as if nothing had happened.

Sun shone through the stained-glass windows, casting beautiful ghostly patterns on the wooden pews and the dark grey habits of the nuns.

Tiptoeing again, we entered and stood at the back waiting for the chanting to finish. It lasted another ten minutes, then the nun at the front, who we learned was Mother Superior, turned to us. She had no laugher lines round her eyes, and her mouth was set in a line as firm as the stone of the building.

'Back to your tasks,' she said to the gathered nuns, about twenty of them. Then she strode towards us without the remotest change of expression on her face.

'How can I help you?' she said, although her tone suggested that helping us was the last thing she wanted to do.

I let Amanda do the talking. Her French was so much better than mine and I felt this stern woman wouldn't be impressed by my English accent.

'We found this child, Elise, at the railway station. She has become separated from her family. We need to go to Dunkirk urgently but have to find someone to take care of her.'

The Mother Superior peered at Elise, a frown on her face. She held the large wooden cross she wore on a rope round her neck. 'Bless you, my child,' she said with a lack of warmth that belied her words. 'Where do you come from?'

Elise's reply was to suck her thumb harder and hide behind Mavis's legs.

Amanda spoke up again. 'She doesn't say anything other than her name. We have asked around the village where we spent last night and no one knows her there. We heard you take in children.'

Mother Superior raised her eyes to heaven. 'We do – children of fallen women who should know better than to bring an unwanted child into the world.'

'But...' I spluttered, 'maybe they do want them but can't keep them.'

Her lip curled. 'Then they should have kept their legs together, young lady, as all of you should.'

I stared at her in amazement. How could someone who claimed to be a Christian be so cold and unfeeling? I heard my pulse in my ears as I fought not to respond rudely.

'Are you suggesting...?' I started.

Amanda reached over and held my arm. 'Mother Superior. Can you help us? We really have to go to Dunkirk urgently.'

She gave an exaggerated sigh. 'Follow me,' she commanded, putting her hands inside her sleeves and walking with a back as rigid as a brick wall.

We followed her through beautiful carved cloisters. In the middle of the square was a fountain, not apparently working. Four children, about ten years old, were weeding the garden. They were shabbily dressed and all had hair shaved to within half an inch of their skull. They spoke not a word, nor did they look up as we passed.

'As you can see, we teach the children valuable skills,' Mother Superior said as we walked past.

Only then did it occur to me that we hadn't heard any sign that there were children living there. No sound, no laughter.

We passed a laundry room. It was a hot day, and the room was small with a wood-fired hot water heater in one corner. Even walking past, we felt the heat radiating from the room. Two big tubs of water stood to one side and a mangle on the opposite wall. Drying racks hung from the ceiling. More children, a little older, shaven and dressed like the gardeners, were washing clothes supervised by a nun who was standing over them without speaking. As we passed, we heard her hiss, 'Not like that, you idiot. Concentrate on the collar.' The sound of a slap soon followed.

'We can't leave Elise here,' I whispered to Amanda, but she walked straight ahead, as unbending as the Mother Superior.

Bronwyn moved to walk next to me. 'We're going to have trouble getting Amanda to agree with you. She's determined to move on quickly, no matter what.'

We hurried to catch up with the others, down cool corridors with heavy wooden doors at regular intervals. Through a window we caught sight of a nun supervising more children, this time working on a vegetable plot. Just when I thought we were going round in circles, Mother Superior took a large key out of her pocket and unlocked a door. Wooden like the others, it had heavy metal hinges and screws, with a gleaming crucifix at eye level.

'Follow me!' she ordered.

We went in, Amanda confidently, the rest of us tentatively, treading lightly on the ancient stones. I felt as if I were walking into the devil's lair. Dark wood bookshelves lined one wall, while a side table and battered filing cabinet stood opposite.

Mother Superior sat down behind an enormous wooden desk. A neat pile of letters was in front of her and a pen and pencil lined up exactly beside them. A crucifix on a stand was on one corner. The only other things on the desk were a blotting pad and a bottle of ink. We were not invited to sit down.

She picked up a pen. 'Name!' she ordered.

'Who's name?' I asked.

Her lips tightened to a straight line. 'The child's name, of course, and I'll need her date of birth and other details, too.'

'But we explained, the only thing we know about her is that her name is Elise.'

She looked at me, then at Elise.

'You! Come here!' She beckoned with her index finger.

Elise whimpered and clutched my leg tightly. There was a pause, then, 'I said, come here!'

'Maybe a little later,' I said.

She tapped her pen against the desk. 'Who's going to pay for her keep?' she asked.

Amanda stepped forward. 'We can't do that, we are heading back to England. As I explained, we just found this girl at the station, we've never met her before. You have to take her in, we need to go.'

Mother Superior gave a heavy sigh. 'Well, I suppose another bastard child...'

She didn't get to finish her sentence. I grabbed Elise's hand. 'I don't know how you can call yourself a Christian, you cold-hearted woman. God will punish you for the way you behave. I wouldn't leave a dog with you, much less a child!'

And with that I stormed out of the room, pulling Elise behind me. The trouble was, once I was outside the door I had no idea how to get out of the building or even if the others would back me up. I stood and stamped my foot like a two-year-old, fighting off tears. Elise held her hands up, tears running down her grubby face, wanting a cuddle, but not as much as I did. I was just beginning to think I'd been deserted when the door opened again and the others joined me in the corridor. Behind them, the door slammed with a bang loud enough to be heard a mile away.

We walked back the way we'd come, as if we knew what we were doing.

'You are bloody crazy!' Amanda hissed, stopping me in my tracks. I'd never heard her swear before, never mind so violently. 'We may die trying to save this girl. Is that what you want?'

Elise's sobs became louder and her entire body began to shake.

I looked to the others. Bronwyn avoided my eye. 'She's got a point,' she said, 'the Germans could be here any time, we need to be gone.'

I stopped still. 'You can do what you want, all of you. Go ahead without me if you like, but I am going to make sure this little girl is somewhere safe. Is that clear?'

It was Mavis, impulsive Mavis, who calmed us down. 'Let's stop this now, girls,' she said in a voice gentle enough to begin to calm Elise's shakes. 'Let's try one more village and if we can't find anyone who knows her, we'll leave Elise with the vicar. He'll have to find someone.'

She looked at us all. 'Agreed?'

Bronwyn nodded and after a minute Amanda said, 'Oh, come on then, if you all insist, but do hurry!'

* * *

Luck was with us, and the same van that gave us a lift before caught up with us before we'd gone five hundred yards.

'Where are you off to now, my lovelies?' Pierre asked.

We hadn't a clue where to ask for. 'Is there a nearby village that's on the way to the railway station?' Mavis asked. 'Not the one we came from. We need to find someone who can take care of this little girl.'

A mere twenty minutes later we pulled into the next village. Unlike the last one, the streets were crowded with people walking in the same direction with heavy feet and weary backs. They carried their most precious belongings and walked determinedly, putting one foot before the other; concentrating, afraid.

We knocked on the first door we came to without much hope. A curtain twitched, then a minute later the door opened a crack. A thin, middle-aged woman peered out, eyes narrowed. Then she noticed Elise, who was back in my arms.

'Elise!' she said. 'What on earth are you doing here? Why aren't you with your mother?'

A huge sigh escaped from Elise. She held out her arms to the woman. 'Auntie,' she said, 'I'm hungry.'

We looked from one to the other with amazement.

Soon we were on our way again, without Elise but with a cheese baguette each.

13

DASH FOR THE COAST

'Where to now, then?' Bronwyn asked as we set off after leaving Elise with her aunt.

'Yeah, 'ow the 'ell are we going to get to Dunkirk?' Mavis asked as we headed back towards the station. 'We don't even know where the trains from 'ere go. If it's back to Paris, that's way too dangerous.'

'To tell you the truth, I don't know how we can even find out where the Germans have got to. Surely to goodness, the further north we go the more likely we are to bump into them.'

Our spirits sank. Bronwyn was right. We walked silently for a couple of minutes, going in the opposite direction to the tide of weary refugees.

'We're stupid,' I said, smacking myself on the forehead, 'let's ask the refugees we're passing. They must have some idea.'

'But they may all 'ave different ideas 'cos they've come by different routes,' Mavis said.

Amanda pursed her lips – something she'd been doing with increasing frequency for the past couple of days. Stress was getting to us all, making us short tempered and snappy. 'Lily's right,' she said. 'It's our only option. If we ask enough, we'll get a general picture. Has anyone got a better idea?'

We asked half a dozen people and got different answers, but it seemed most likely that the Germans had got as far south as Abbeville.

That stopped us in our tracks.

'God, that's miles further south than Dunkirk. If the Germans hold all that region, how the hell do we get through?'

'She's right,' Bronwyn said. 'Maybe we should go south instead.'

I shook my head. 'But how would we get over to England then? It would be a longer journey by sea and we may get sunk or anything. Let's think this over. The Germans can't be on every single road and we were told we could evacuate from Dunkirk.'

'And we can pass off as Frenchwomen,' Amanda joined in, sounding more positive. 'After all, the Germans won't be familiar with every French accent. We'd have to be careful to speak to each other only in French if there's anyone else about though.'

We spent another ten minutes trying to think of a better plan, but ended up deciding to get to Dunkirk as quickly as possible, all the while pretending to be Frenchwomen. 'We can say we went south with all the other evacuees but decided to go back home after all.' I added. None of us had a better plan.

We still had miles and miles to travel.

We went back to the station we'd arrived at where we found Elise. We'd heard the Germans were bombing stations and were relieved to find it hadn't been damaged. A train in the right direction was due in an hour. Two and a half hours later it arrived, emptier than the ones going south, so we managed to get seats. Amanda, always the organised one, had a map of France in her bag and studied it as we set off. Twice we had to get out because part of the track had been bombed. Along with other passengers we walked alongside the missing track until we found another train. It was a slow, tiring journey.

Eventually, we arrived at a station about fifty miles in roughly the right direction. Still a long way to go but better than nothing.

Our food long gone, we went into the nearby town and were grateful to find a café open. It was crowded with refugees trying to stock up for the rest of their trek. The air was filled with the smell of sweat, onions and desperation.

The waiter tried to smile as he greeted us, but was too worn out to make a good job of it.

'I only have cheese baguettes.' He indicated a pile of half-size baguettes inside a glass cabinet. 'We've filled that twice this morning. In another ten minutes there will be none left.'

'Eight, please, two for each of us.' I was getting my purse out.

'No! Greedy girls!' someone shouted. 'One each!'

'One each!'

The waiter put four baguettes in a bag. 'One each is the rule, there's not enough to go round.'

He charged three times the usual price.

'What now?' Bronwyn asked, as we left the café, her chin quivering a little. 'How the hell are we going to get the rest of the way? We might be going right into enemy territory.'

We were stuck for alternatives. No train went in the right direction until the next day.

'Let's walk and see if we can get a lift, or a series of lifts if people can only take us part of the way.'

We got one lift with a delivery van. The driver, Hugo, told us horror stories of women who travelled with French soldiers for protection, being raped by them.

Hearing that, I caught my breath and put my hand to my chest. 'Surely soldiers wouldn't do that.'

His mouth twisted. 'In these times people are not themselves.

They do things they would never do normally. You girls must be very careful. There may be four of you, but there are many more soldiers.'

Feeling very shaken we thanked him for his kindness and started walking again, checking around us constantly.

We tried, as much as possible, to keep to country lanes or even walk across fields because of the sheer volume of refugees on the road. We were going in the opposite direction to most of them although some were going the same way as us. We caught snatches of conversations, and alarming rumours. 'The Germans fight in shirtsleeves!' 'They're only five kilometres behind us!' 'The Belgians have abandoned us!' 'The British are going back home!'

'I don't mean to be funny or nothing,' Bronwyn said, 'but I don't think we can believe any of this. How would they know? There's no newspapers or anything. It's just people trying to make themselves important pretending to know something. See how everyone crowds around them.'

Amanda nodded. 'I wonder if some of them are Fifth Columnists wanting to spread alarm. People have been abandoned by the authorities, no wonder they sound bitter. And, they think anyone with a big car is a Jew.'

I gestured towards a house we'd just passed. 'There was a radio in there. Some people might have listened to the news while they were looting places. But who knows if the news came from the French or the Germans?'

'You're right,' Amanda said. 'I heard some people saying Radio Stuttgart keeps announcing how successful the invasion is and telling people to leave their homes. The Germans are probably giving false information to get people out of their villages and further south. It would make it a lot easier for them to gain territory. There'd be no resistance whatsoever.'

Further on, we caught up with a middle-aged man who was

pulling a heavily laden cart. Sweat ran from under his flat cap and his entire body sagged under the terrific weight he was pulling. The screeching metal wheels had no tyres. Rolls of bedding, saucepans, suitcases and bundles balanced precariously were barely kept in place by string. Behind the cart, five children aged between about seven and eleven pushed as he pulled.

'Where are you going, Monsieur?' we asked. 'Everyone else is going the other way.'

He stopped and put down his burden for a moment, groaning with relief. The children, relieved of their task too, sat on the road and started to play jacks. Their father got out a grubby handkerchief and wiped his face. 'Back home. We're going back home. There is nothing ahead for anyone. No food. Some towns have closed off their centre and make you walk the long way. One farmer even charged me a fortune for a jug of water. Bastard!' He tried to spit to show his disgust, but his mouth was too dry. He nodded towards the people still heading south. 'They'll be turning back by tomorrow, just you wait and see.'

We were about to ask him for more information when we heard the distinctive woo-woo-woo of German planes approaching from the north. 'Quick! Take cover!' someone shouted. 'They'll kill us.'

The planes were on us before we could think, their shadows darkening the skies. Like everyone else, we dived into the ditches next to the trees, our hands covering our heads. We saw parents throw themselves over their children, others pinned themselves to a tree or stood with their hands over their heads helplessly. The air was full of screams and the terrifying roar of the planes and the bullets bouncing off the road or sometimes the dull thud as they hit people or mattresses. I have never been so scared in my life. I cowered there on the wet ground, twigs pressing against my face. I tried to breathe but it was as if my lungs had forgotten how to work and my heart thumped so loudly surely everyone would hear it. I saw the mouths of people nearby as they prayed or screamed or reassured their loved ones, but heard nothing but my heartbeat and the cruel sound of the engines.

It seemed only the children breathed; too unknowing to be frightened. Some laughed, thinking it was a game of Cowboys and Indians. The adults held their breath, and in many cases crossed themselves and prayed. When we dared to look back, we found the people on foot had had an advantage over those in cars. In the few precious seconds it took some of them to get out of their vehicle to relative safety, they were gunned down. Cars had bullet holes, blood on the seats and sometimes bodies hanging half out of the car or still in the back seats.

When the planes had gone and people started to get back on the road, we saw a man holding the lifeless body of a five-year-old girl in his arms, her blonde hair trailing from her limp head, a blue ribbon dragging on the ground. Her chest was a mass of blood and the man sobbed as if his heart would break. 'Does anyone know where there's a cemetery?' he called, over and over and over again.

We saw a boy whose shoulder was fractured by a bullet. Trying to be brave, he was biting his bottom lip so hard it was white. There was a woman in a car with three children. She hardly knew how to drive, numb with grief. 'My husband was killed yesterday, I've never driven before, but we must escape.' Her children sat silently in the back seat, their faces white as flour, eyes red-rimmed.

Gradually, the columns of people re-formed, some carrying their dead, others leaving them under the trees. No one spoke, though the sound of sobs was something I knew I'd never forget. The smell of dirt and engines and blood filled the air.

A little further on, we met up again with the man with the cart and helped him pull it to the next turn-off, where we left him with many hugs and good wishes.

We walked along a quiet country road where there was little traffic. We were so lost in our own thoughts and the memories of the horrors we'd just seen we barely spoke, but plodded on, unaware of the lovely countryside around us.

Trees lined one side of the road giving us shade, and the other side bordered a field edged with wild flowers. Poppies, daisies and herb robert swayed in the breeze, unseen and ignorant of the chaos surrounding them. As we walked, a branch of lilac brushed against my face, its heady scent bringing me out my trance.

After ten minutes, Amanda put up her hand. 'Let's just go round the next corner, then we'll stop and rest.'

Bronwyn nodded, 'I'm just going behind that tree for a wee. Won't be a minute. Don't wait for me, I'll catch you up.'

14

THE EMPTY CAR

We walked slowly on, and round the corner saw an apparently empty Citroën car. 'Blimey,' Mavis said, 'an empty car. They're like gold dust what with the evacuation. Think we should nick it?'

'It's probably run out of petrol and been dumped.'

'Don't be so negative!' She gave me a mock punch on the arm.

I rubbed my arm, pretending to be in pain. 'Know how to start one without keys?'

Bronwyn chipped in, 'I do. Didn't have a misspent youth for nothing. We can take it if it's got any petrol. Save a lot of walking.'

'But then we'd be thieves.'

'So what? Needs must.'

We continued to walk towards it. 'Can you see anyone in it?' Mavis whispered as we got nearer.

I peered around through the trees. 'I expect the driver's having a wee, too. He'll probably be back any minute. But let's be careful, there are a lot of desperate people about now.'

Amanda drew a breath and looked around too. 'I don't think there's anyone here. Perhaps it's broken down and they dumped it. It's pretty old.'

Without quite knowing why, we edged slowly towards the car. A crow nearby let out a shrill alarm cry, and a breeze sprung up from nowhere.

We were almost at the car when we saw something that made us stop in our tracks.

A German soldier was lying on the back seat, his eyes closed.

As one, we turned to run.

Then something terrifying happened.

My rucksack banged on the side of the car and the soldier woke up. The crow screamed again and flew over our heads, wings flapping noisily.

The soldier opened his eyes, took one look at us, his eyes widened, then he reached for the gun in his pocket, shouting loudly.

I didn't understand what he was saying, but the gun pointing at us was clear enough.

We put our hands in the air and started to edge away. He climbed out of the car, keeping his eyes firmly on us. Gesturing with the gun, he indicated we should stand by the side of the road near the trees.

His eyes roamed over us, stopping at Amanda. Her long blonde hair was coming unpinned and fell in loose curls around her face and shoulders. She was dishevelled but still attractive, a fine film of sweat on her forehead. He licked his lips as he looked her up and down, a leer on his face. As I saw that, my heart sank and I feared for her and all of us.

Mavis was quietly rocking on her feet. 'Do you think he wants our bodies in the ditch so he can drive off without the worry of moving us?'

'I'm more worried about what he wants to do with our bodies while we're alive,' I replied.

She blinked and jerked back her head. 'Bloody hell! The

bastard. What shall we do? Try to take him? He can't rape us all at the same time. Or shoot us.'

The soldier's voice became more urgent, more; aggressive. He stamped his foot and started waving his gun wildly: his eyes vicious and narrowed.

'Amanda, you speak some German, what's he saying?'

'I can't tell, I don't understand his accent, but whatever it is it's not good. He keeps saying "Englisch". We should've spoken in French. Where's Bronwyn?'

We were soon to find out.

She was edging her way towards the from behind him, taking every step slowly, trying not to make a sound. Sweat trickled down her forehead. She had a chunky tree branch in her hands.

'Let's all talk loudly so he won't hear her,' I whispered, although I was pretty sure he didn't understand English.

'Don't kill us!' Mavis screeched. 'We're not doing anything wrong. Please! We'll just go!'

'We'll just walk away, no problem,' I said loudly, my voice overlapping Mavis's.

Amanda starting singing 'Frère Jacques' at the top of her voice, and we all turned and gaped at her. It was exactly what Bronwyn had been waiting for. She lunged forward, the branch raised, and our hearts stopped as the soldier heard her and began to turn towards her direction. But he was too late. She swung the branch with all her might and brought it down on the side of his head with a loud crack. He collapsed sideways, his head hitting a large stone as he fell.

Blood started to pool around his head. He didn't move or open his eyes.

I ran forward and grabbed his gun, pointing it towards him, my hands shaking so much I'd never have hit him in a million years.

'Don't move!' I said stupidly. It's not as if he could hear me.

'Let's steal his car before he wakes up.' Mavis had a wicked smile on her face. 'I'll see if the keys are in the ignition.' She turned towards the car, but Amanda's voice stopped her.

Avoiding the growing pool of blood on the ground, she bent down beside the soldier, and felt his neck. 'I don't think he's going to wake up. There is no pulse.'

We stood blinking in disbelief.

'You mean... You mean... he's dead?' Bronwyn said. 'I killed him?'

She staggered and grabbed my arm, her breath coming hard and fast. 'Oh my God, what're we going to do? What if anyone sees us? I'll be hanged for murder!'

I grabbed her shoulder to calm her. 'Shh! Keep your voice down. Let me think.'

'Anyone know how to try to bring him back to life?'

'We'd have to act fast,' Amanda's said. 'I read you should press on his chest and lift his arm. The thing is, do we want to save him?' She raised an eyebrow.

'But... but... we can't just let him die.' Bronwyn was so agitated she was moving from one foot to the other non-stop.

'Too late, he's already dead,' I said, my voice squeaky. 'I say, let's leave him dead. He's the enemy.'

'Can we... should we... we didn't mean...' Bronwyn's words tumbled over each other.

I stood opposite her and held her shoulders. 'That's right, Bronwyn. You did the right thing. You saved our lives. Now, let's see if he's got anything useful in his pockets.'

Turning him this way and that, I searched his clothes. The first thing I found was a photo of a pretty girl about the soldier's age. 'I wonder if that's his sister or girlfriend,' I said. I put the photo back in his pocket, and felt around some more. I took out some money and the car keys, along with a bar of chocolate and some cigarettes.

'Got to get him out of sight,' I muttered, 'come and help me move him.'

Mavis moved towards me. 'Right, I'll move his top half, you do his legs.'

We started to roll the soldier away from the road, streaks of blood following his path. He was quite slight but awkward to move. I hated the feel of his uniform and the iron smell of his blood. It only took a moment or two and he was in a ditch at the side of the road by the trees. The trouble was, he was still visible from the road.

'Let's cover him with foliage,' I said. Mavis was already bending down to find suitable branches. That took another few minutes. It wasn't much of a hiding place, but on this deserted stretch of road and with the thick trees hiding him, it was unlikely anyone would find him unless they were walking their dog or something.

Amanda was comforting Bronwyn, but watching what we were doing. She pointed to the road. 'What about the blood? It'd be easy to see. Find a branch and cover that up, too.'

There was a couple of inches of water in the ditch so I got a branch with some leaves on, soaked it and tried to make the blood less obvious. It took several goes and all the time we were watching out for traffic coming along. Eventually, we were satisfied no one would notice.

I dusted my hands and clothes and took Bronwyn by the arm, my tone brisk. 'Come on, Bronwyn, you'll be fine. That's one less Nazi to kill our soldiers – or us. You're a hero, remember that. You saved our lives and probably saved Amanda from being raped too. Now, Amanda, am I right in thinking you can drive?'

She nodded. 'I've never driven a car like that, but I'm sure I'll manage.'

'Right, let's get in the car and as far away from here as quickly as we can.'

They followed like lambs, too weary to argue. I was surprised at the way I was bossing them around, although my old manager at the Dream Palace would have said I was displaying leadership qualities.

Amanda turned the key, and the engine started first time. 'Three-quarters of a tank,' she muttered. 'Right, this is what I'm going to do. I'm going to drive us the way we were going just long enough to find somewhere away from here in case someone comes searching for him. We'll hide up while I study the map then be on our way. If there is anything that shows the car belonged to the German, chuck it unless we can use it. Okay?'

Bronwyn was still in a state of shock. Head in her hands, she kept repeating, 'He's dead, I killed him.' No amount of us telling her she saved our lives stopped her shaking.

We were desperate with the need to calm her, then out of the blue Mavis asked her, 'What's the nicest place you've been to in Wales?'

I thought she'd gone mad. I gave her a 'what's that got to do with anything?' look, but she ignored me.

The question seemed to shake Bronwyn out of her guilt trance. 'I... I...' she started, then looked up as if seeing us and her surroundings for the first time. 'The Mumbles – best beach in the world. Probably covered in barbed wire now though.'

We kept her chatting about happy memories until we were convinced she was back in control. We needed to – we were likely to face a lot of dangers in the next few hours or days.

Amanda's map-reading skills saved the day. We stuck to small roads and went through deserted village after deserted village. Houses had been looted, many doors left open. Several times we saw people coming out of houses with bags or even pillowcases stuffed with things they'd just stolen. Sometimes it was French soldiers doing the looting.

'Should we nick some stuff?' Mavis said. 'Germans will get it otherwise.'

At first we resisted, but as the hours went by and we grew hungry and thirsty, we gave into temptation. There was precious little left because hordes of refugees going in the opposite direction had got there first. But we got water from a pump in someone's garden and some not-quite-ripe fruit off a couple of trees.

Finally, we went into a house where the door was already open. We searched through the kitchen and larder but it had been completely stripped, even the dry goods had gone.

Amanda closed the larder door. 'If that man with the cart is right and people turn back, they'll have nothing to eat.'

Bronwyn nodded. 'Nothing in the shops either.'

'Whatever will people do, they'll be desperate.'

Although we passed many refugees, mostly going in the opposite direction, we met no German troops. It was a squeeze but we were able to give an elderly couple who were returning home a lift to their village. They invited us in for the night and we gratefully accepted. Like so many others, their kitchen had been emptied by looters. With trembling chins they tidied up, then shuffled into their garden. Their chickens were still there and they found four eggs under the straw. The vegetable patch had been trampled on by the looters, but they managed to rescue a few early potatoes and some carrots. We shared the chocolate we'd taken from the German, and had a humble meal we were very thankful for.

Amanda checked the dashboard, her face gloomy. 'I don't want to depress you, girls, but we're almost out of petrol.'

My heart jumped a beat. 'Any idea how far we've got to go?'

'How much petrol left?' Bronwyn asked.

Amanda winced. 'It's only a guess but I think we've still got about fifty-five miles to go. I doubt the petrol will get us even twenty miles.'

Her voice was cut off by the sound of gunfire. Skidding loudly, Amanda drove the car into the shelter of some trees and we lay low until it subsided before venturing out again.

Waiting for the petrol to run out was agonising. We constantly peered over Amanda's shoulder at the gauge or irritated her by asking how much further she thought we'd get.

When the tank was finally empty and we ground to a halt, we wearily put on our rucksacks and started walking again – hungry and thirsty.

15

THE RED CROSS

Five miles further on, we saw a sight that lifted our spirits. Two Red Cross ambulances. Finding energy we didn't know we had, we flagged one of them down. The driver hung out of the window and shouted, 'No lifts, we're full.'

'But we're ATS!' we called back. 'We were stationed in Paris and got lost getting to Dunkirk.'

He gave a grunt. 'How do I know you're telling the truth? We can't just take anyone you know. We're chock-a-block as it is.'

We'd all kept our identity papers, intending to dump them at the first sign of being captured. Now we showed them to him and waited while he inspected them. With a frown he gestured to the passenger door. 'Get in, it'll be a squeeze though.'

He was right, there was already someone in there, a soldier with his leg in plaster and another with a bandage over one eye and his arm in a sling. They were completely done in. Nonetheless, they seemed a little livelier when they saw us. 'Hello, sweetheart,' one of them said, 'where've you been all my life?'

Mavis gave him a cheeky grin back. 'Waiting for you, you gorgeous 'unk.'

We had to sit on each other's knees, but the relief of having a lift more than made up for it. It was such bliss to speak to other English people and to get off our feet.

'How far have you come?' we asked the driver, who said his name was Fred.

He raised his eyes to heaven. 'Not far if we'd been able to go direct, like. But we got halted by a military policeman 'cos Amiens was being shelled by Germans advancing from the east, so we couldn't get to Dieppe. Gotta get to Boulogne before that falls too.'

'We were told to go to Dunkirk,' I explained, 'but that was days ago, so I expect everything's changed. What do you think we should do?'

The bandaged soldier spoke up. 'I heard there's a mass evacuation of troops from Dunkirk and along there, but it's bloody dangerous, excuse my language. There's loads of boats, big and small, trying to get the men away but the bloody Germans are giving them hell; even bombing hospital ships. And they say the beaches are littered with bodies.'

Fred nodded. 'That's about right. Dangerous to go and even more dangerous to stay. We're heading towards the ambulance trains not far from here. But I doubt they'll be safe if the bastards are bombing the Red Cross ships. Still, gotta try, ain't you?'

The bandaged soldier spoke again. 'I heard even if they're not bombed, half the tracks are up. And doctors trying to operate in all that. They deserve a chest full of medals, they do. Nurses, too.'

Half an hour later, we reached the rendezvous point. It was organised chaos. All sorts of vehicles were offloading the wounded, and nurses and doctors assessed them by the side of the road, trying to give each the time they required, but all the time checking round for those in more urgent need. Those who had died on the journey were gently laid to one side while the staff attended to the living. Kind words mingled with cries of pain and pleas for help. Unskilled as we were, we helped as best we could, mostly standing by to give bandages to doctors or take soiled ones and disposing of them. It was an hour before we got on an ambulance train and it started to slowly pull away from the station.

I went over to one of the nurses. 'We're ATS. What can we do to help?'

She was hastily bandaging a soldier's head. 'There's plenty of tidying and cleaning to do, but make sure you don't get in the way.'

Now the smell of blood we'd experienced too much of in recent days mingled with the smell of unwashed bodies, disinfectant and putrefying flesh. The carriage windows only opened a little way, so not much fresh air reached us.

The carriage was so cramped we constantly got in each other's way and I sometimes wondered if we were more help than hindrance. But the nurses, exhausted as they were, were polite when they gave us instructions on what to do next.

I was helping one nurse, Nurse Tomkinson, her badge said, when she looked up from bandaging a man's foot, and said, 'Back in a minute.' To my amazement, she got up and jumped from one carriage to the next. At any minute she was in danger of falling between carriages and being killed.

'You didn't see that,' one of the other nurses said. 'It's strictly forbidden, but...' She shrugged her shoulders and turned back to her work, 'come with me.' She led me to where a doctor was operating. The smell of rotting flesh got stronger with each step. I reeled back in horror when I noticed the saw in the doctor's hand. He glanced at me, probably noticed me going green as I tried not to breathe in the awful smell. 'Right, it's your job to help the nurse. We've got to amputate this man's leg. If you're going to faint, fall backwards.'

'This should never have happened,' the nurse said as we worked. 'Whoever put the tourniquet on him should have released it regularly to allow the blood to flow. But it's too late now.' She lowered her voice. 'He probably won't make it, but you've got to try, haven't you.'

We reached the town of Albert when the train screeched to a halt. 'Track's blown up,' was the word that quickly spread down the train. The sound of a plane approaching and an almighty bang told us that the track had just been blown up the other way. For a second we all stood still as statues wondering what to do; the train was stranded and many of the casualties couldn't walk.

Very quickly someone, who we learned was the Commanding Officer, walked round. 'Right!' he said, his voice brooking no nonsense. 'You nurses get off the train. The French railway workers will give you directions as best they can. They're waiting outside for you. Sorry I haven't got any transport to offer you. No arguments, just get away.'

'But what about the wounded?' someone asked.

'No arguments, they're my responsibility. Just get off. Now!' he said, his voice harsh and stressed. The nurses hurriedly grabbed their essentials and we joined them on what turned out to be a long journey.

Although it took us seven long days to get to Cherbourg, the port we were told to embark from, we had quite a jolly time despite the danger. There were five nurses and us four. Relieved of their heartbreaking work, they gradually let go of their stress and we had lots of laughs. After the difficult time we'd all had it was a real tonic.

We spent one night in a barn, sharing the space with cows. After the smell of sickness on the train, we barely noticed their smell. And we walked so far each day, we fell into a deep sleep almost as soon as we lay down.

On the second day, we heard gunfire and had no way of knowing where the front was. We hid until it stopped and then, taking care to keep under the cover of trees, continued on our way, cautious, fearful, tentative.

For two days we had nothing to eat although we were lucky enough to find an empty farmhouse where the water pump still worked. We spent the night there in relative comfort. Of course, all the food had been taken by looters, but some vegetables were ready to be picked and we made ourselves a vegetable stew. Rarely had anything tasted so good. For dessert we found some nearly ripe fruit in the trees.

We'd left the farmhouse and were walking along a quiet lane when a horse and cart came bumping along. We'd been so busy chatting we didn't hear it coming or have time to hide. Luck was with us, it was a local farmer.

'You girls need a lift?' he called. 'You look all hot and bothered. Come on, hop in the back.' It was a squash with so many of us but no one minded.

'Have you got any idea where the fighting is going on?' I asked, raising my voice above the sound of the wooden wheels.

He gave a bitter laugh. 'Wish I knew. It seems to change every day. I just keep my eyes open and hide whenever I hear any fighting. I expect you do the same. Where are you girls going?'

'Cherbourg,' I replied, then wondered if I should have told him. I'd been so well trained in keeping mum about information it was hard to tell anyone anything at times.

'Ah, well, then,' he said, 'I won't be a lot of use to you. I'm going about five or six kilometres in your direction, then you'll be on your own. Tell you what, though, it's not much, but I can give you a baguette to see you on your way.' He leaned across and pulled one out of a hessian back, and passed it back to us. When he finally dropped us off, we all kissed him gratefully.

Our next lift was with a Salvation Army canteen van.

The rest of our journey passed in much the same way. Periods of hunger interspersed with getting small amounts to eat; walking, walking and more walking; hiding from gunfire; enjoying walking along sunny lanes. Amanda, bless her heart, still had her map and an instinctive knowledge of which way was north. She guided us.

We couldn't believe our eyes when we realised we were finally at Cherbourg. A British army truck found us and drove us to the beach, saving us from walking the final mile or so.

'I'm going to kiss the ground,' Mavis said when we climbed down from the truck, 'and blimey, there's a British ship there.'

I bit my lip. 'But there's stacks of people trying to get on, not just soldiers but civilians. They're all pushing and shoving to get a place.'

The matron, who we'd got to know well on the journey, took control. 'Follow me. They'll let us on when they know who we are.'

Soldiers with fixed bayonets were keeping control of the crowd, and just like Matron said, they let us through. We wished we had our uniforms on as the nurses had. They would have explained to the desperate crowds trying to get on the ships why we were getting preferential treatment.

'I feel just awful getting ahead of all these people,' Bronwyn said, trying not to look anyone in the eye.

We ran down the iron staircase, desperate to get below, our feet clanging and echoing around the hospital ship. It was only when we got to the bottom of the steps that I calmed down enough to take in the scene around me.

Every square inch was filled with men in uniform. Army, air force, navy and one or two not in uniform at all. Many were sitting on the benches against the walls, others sat or lay on the floor dazed. Quite a few were drenched from having fallen in the sea before they were rescued. A couple wolf-whistled or made suggestive remarks, but most didn't have the energy.

The room was full of smells: blood, oil, unwashed bodies, seawater and fear all fought to invade our senses.

'Not being funny or nothing,' Bronwyn said, 'but what the hell are we supposed to do now?'

The nurses we'd travelled with immediately set to, confidently helping the men, moving among them comforting; adjusting dressings and noting who needed urgent help. I envied their skills.

'Just get stuck in. You've had a bit of practice now,' one of them shouted to us over her shoulder as she moved towards a man who was bleeding profusely.

A soldier with blood running down one arm tried to smile at me, but it came out more as a grimace. His face and uniform were splattered with seawater and drying sand which dropped to the floor as he moved. 'What're you girls doing here? You civvies?'

'ATS,' I said, 'thought we'd better ditch our uniforms in case we got captured.'

'Well, you're lucky, there's a rumour this is the last ship from Cherbourg. But I 'eard they've got thousands of men 'ome safe and sound. Let's 'ope we'll get there too.'

A door on the opposite wall opened with a clatter and a doctor came in. He was wearing an operating gown splattered with blood. His hair was sticking up at all angles, his face was pallid, and his forehead lined with wrinkles. He walked around, stepping carefully to avoid treading on the exhausted men, and stopping each time he came to someone who was groaning, bloodstained or unconscious. Some men tried to grab his leg or hand, begging for something for their pain.

He turned to two orderlies who'd come with him.

'Take him—' he pointed '—and him, and him. The rest of you who have injuries, I'm sorry about the wait. Let us know if your condition changes drastically. We won't be that long getting to Dover, so chin up.'

'Come on,' Mavis said, 'let's see what we can do to 'elp. It'll take our minds off things.'

I nodded. 'We could all do with a good cup of tea to calm our nerves but come on, let's see if we can help. Our nurse friends will tell us what to do. Mind you, I'm rather inclined to faint at the sight of blood even now.'

The soldier who'd been speaking before piped up, 'Well, in that case a hospital ship wasn't the best choice for you, was it, sweetheart?'

I went back up a couple of steps to get a better view of the men. 'Hoping to find Edward?' Bronwyn asked. 'He's still a prisoner of war, isn't he?'

'Mmm, I'm not sure. We haven't heard from him for ages, and prisoners should be allowed to write. But it's probably the Germans being awkward. Anyway, there's no harm looking. He might have escaped. Anything could have happened to him.'

With a heavy heart, I went back down the steps. The engines started and the ship grumbled and creaked as we got underway. I headed towards a soldier who was groaning. I took his hand, unsure what to do. Should I talk about his injury or try to distract him?

'Hello, I'm Lily,' I said, 'what's your name?'

'Jim. You're a sight for sore eyes, miss.' Wincing, he squeezed my hand. 'Been shot in the arm,' he said, although that was easy to see from his bloodstained clothes, 'one of the lucky ones, two of my mates didn't make it.'

'I'm so sorry, that's awful.' I stroked his good hand. 'I wish I could take the pain away for you.'

'Seeing your face is a pretty good tonic, I can tell you. Takes me mind off it.'

A shuddering and clanging shook the ship. He stopped and listened. 'Sounds like we're making up for lost time, thank Christ for that,' he said. 'The bastards ain't supposed to bomb 'ospital ships, but we 'eard they do.'

I went cold. 'You mean we might still be sunk?'

He nodded, flinching as the movement hurt his injury. 'Sure as eggs is eggs we can. Torpedoed, bombed by planes, who knows what. But we got this far, luck's on our side.'

Just then a man nearby started to groan more loudly. 'Excuse me, Jim, I'm just going to see that soldier over there.'

I stepped carefully between the legs of half a dozen men sitting on the floor and squatted down next to the groaning soldier. His eyes were closed, his face ashen, his lips turning blue, and his breathing shallow and rapid.

'I'm Lily,' I said, taking his hands. His injury wasn't obvious, but it was clear he was in a lot of pain. He opened his eyes but they were far away. 'Tell my wife... I...' he said, then stopped and all the tension was gone out of him and he relaxed. Relieved for him, I was just about to go to someone else when an awful thought struck me. I put my hand under his nose. There was no breath. His life had slipped away quietly and his wife would never know what he had to tell her. Yet another woman just made a widow.

Bronwyn caught my eyes from a little way away. 'Gone?' she mouthed. I nodded, tears slowly making traces in the grime on my cheeks.

'Go on, girl, get on to the next one. You can't give comfort to the dead.'

For the rest of the journey the four of us moved around, supporting the nurses when they told us what to do. Each time the engine noise changed, my heart skipped a beat, but eventually we heard a cry, 'Dover in sight!' I nearly wept. Not just for me but for all the men we left behind and all our troops risking their lives for our country.

A cheer went up amongst the men who were well enough to

respond, and some clapped their hands. The air felt lighter as if a great weight, a great threat to us all, had been lifted.

We went on deck to watch the landing. The weather was good, sunny with light clouds skimming the blue. We warmed our faces in the sun, the tension of the last few days slowly beginning to drain away, although we realised the memories would never fade. Dover cliffs never appeared whiter. Seagulls flew around the boat, screeching, hoping for scraps. Their noise competed with the sounds of the boat and the sea. Around the ship we saw a lot of smaller boats, many of them damaged.

'That's some of the boats that have been getting the troops back,' one of the crew said.

My eyes widened. 'What, little boats like that?'

He nodded, 'That's right, dozens and dozens of them. Back and forward they've been going. Never intended for that sort of work. Heroes, the lot of them.'

'Did they all make it back?'

His face dropped. 'No, we lost a fair few. They'll never be forgotten.'

He gave us a little salute and walked back into the ship. I blinked away tears at the thought of those men who gave up their lives trying to bring back home soldiers who had risked their own lives to save the country.

As we drew nearer the port, crowds of people waved and shouted cheerfully. We got energy from their excitement and good-will. It seemed to take for ever for us to moor alongside, and the shudder as the boat bumped into the port almost knocked us off our feet.

Before the rocking had stopped, nurses and sailors were queueing to get off with stretcher cases.

'They're more desperate than us,' I said, holding back my

eagerness to be ashore. 'Come on, let's just wave to the crowds as if we know someone.'

Bronwyn immediately started to wave energetically. 'Not likely we'd know anyone, after all we haven't been able to let our families know we were coming back. Still, it'll be a surprise when we walk in the door.'

We were quickly joined by Amanda and Mavis who grinned and waved too, relief showing on their grubby faces.

They say a watched kettle never boils and it seemed as if the queue of injured disembarking would never end. First the stretcher cases, then some in wheelchairs or on crutches and finally the walking wounded. Every person had a story to tell.

Eventually, it was our turn to leave the ship. We picked up our very few belongings and headed to the gangway.

'Well, girls, we made it,' Amanda said, a catch in her voice. 'I thought we were going to have to bring Elise with us at one point. Then what would we have done?'

Mavis grunted. 'Not you, you were determined to get rid of her. But you were right, we 'ad to get going. I'm just glad Lily insisted we find someone safe to leave 'er with when we did. Let's face it, another 'our and we'd still be standing on that beach at Cherbourg with no ship in sight.'

'I hope she and her mum find each other. I don't know about you lot but I'm going to miss Paris,' I said. 'Wonder if we'll ever get back? If Hitler wins this damn war, would we even want to?'

Mavis paused and gave each of us a quick hug. 'I wonder if we'll get posted together. Knowing you three 'as been the best thing that's ever 'appened to me. I'm going to miss you if we get split up.'

I thought about all we'd been through. The hard grind of training, out in all weathers, covered in mud; shouted at by sergeants and rotten food in the mess. The girl who stole my ring, and Bronwyn's name being cleared. Then the good times in Paris, but also the awfulness of Ingrid's suicide. Finally, the escape from Paris and the long journey home.

'We've been through a lot, girls,' I said, 'but we've survived and we've helped the war effort. We'll always be there for each other.'

And there, at the bottom of the gangway, was Miss Perkins, our boss in Paris. It was like a mirage. I couldn't believe my eyes. Unlike us, she was bandbox smart in her uniform. Her eyes moist, she saluted and gave us the biggest smile.

'Welcome home, girls,' she said, opening her arms wide.

ACKNOWLEDGEMENTS

So many people helped me bring this book from idea to reality. My husband, Rick, contributed many plot ideas – Nero's did a roaring trade in coffee as we discussed them. Also, thanks to the many friends who contributed ideas and/or proofread. They are: Jacqui Kemp, Maggie Scott, Fran Johnstone (my writing buddy), and, course, Eve.

ABOUT THE AUTHOR

Patricia McBride is the author of the very popular Lily Baker historical saga series.

Sign up to Patricia McBride's mailing list for news, competitions and updates on future books.

Visit Patricia's website: www.patriciamcbrideauthor.com

Follow Patricia on social media here:

facebook.com/patriciamcbrideauthor

instagram.com/tricia.mcbride.writer

ALSO BY PATRICIA MCBRIDE

The Lily Baker Series

The Button Girls

The Picture House Girls

The Telephone Girls

The Library Girls of the East End Series

The Library Girls of the East End

Sixpence Stories

Introducing Sixpence Stories!

Discover page-turning historical novels from your favourite authors, meet new friends and be transported back in time.

Join our book club Facebook group

https://bit.ly/SixpenceGroup

Sign up to our newsletter

https://bit.ly/SixpenceNews

Boldwood

Boldwood Books is an award-winning fiction publishing company seeking out the best stories from around the world.

Find out more at www.boldwoodbooks.com

Join our reader community for brilliant books, competitions and offers!

Follow us
@BoldwoodBooks
@TheBoldBookClub

Sign up to our weekly
deals newsletter

https://bit.ly/BoldwoodBNewsletter

Printed in Great Britain
by Amazon

39630956R00126